He moved in closer and closer.

Shelly could feel Wayne's presence, a force somehow bigger than his physical body, which was nothing trifling to begin with. Her gaze latched on to his. She couldn't help it. She wanted to look away, but the power and emotional energy in those eyes held her fast.

"You know something, Miss Harriman?"

"What?"

He sat on the desk corner, until his face was just inches from hers. "I think you and me working together is going to prove very interesting."

So did she. But, unlike him, she could also see the danger lurking beneath....

Dear Reader,

Though August is already upon us, we've got yet another month of special 20th anniversary titles sure to prolong your summer reading pleasure.

STORKVILLE, USA, our newest in-line continuity, launches this month with Marie Ferrarella's *Those Matchmaking Babies*. In this four-book series, the discovery of twin babies abandoned on a day care center's doorstep leads to secrets being revealed...and unsuspecting townsfolk falling in love!

Judy Christenberry rounds up THE CIRCLE K SISTERS with *Cherish the Boss*, in which an old-school cowboy and a modern woman find themselves at odds—and irresistibly attracted to each other! In Cara Colter's memorable VIRGIN BRIDES offering, the "world's oldest living virgin" meets the man she hopes will be her *First Time, Forever.*

Valerie Parv's THE CARRAMER CROWN continues, as a woman long in love with Michel de Marigny poses as *The Prince's Bride-To-Be*. Arlene James delights with *In Want of a Wife*, the story of a self-made millionaire who is looking for a mother for his adopted daughter—and, could it be, a wife for himself? And Natalie Patrick offers the charming *His, Hers...Ours?*, in which a marriage-wary pair play parents and discover they like it—and each other—far too much.

Next month, look for another installment of STORKVILLE, USA, and the launch of THE CHANDLERS REQUEST...from *New York Times* bestselling author Kasey Michaels.

Happy Reading!

Mary-Theresa Hussey

Mary-Theresa Hussey
Senior Editor

Please address questions and book requests to:
Silhouette Reader Service
U.S.: 3010 Walden Ave., P.O. Box 1325, Buffalo, NY 14269
Canadian: P.O. Box 609, Fort Erie, Ont. L2A 5X3

His, Hers...
Ours?

NATALIE PATRICK

Silhouette

R O M A N C E™

Published by Silhouette Books

America's Publisher of Contemporary Romance

For Donna Clayton and Elizabeth Harbison.
You're both great writers
but you're at your best where it really counts, as friends!

SILHOUETTE BOOKS

ISBN 0-373-19467-6

HIS, HERS...OURS?

Books by Natalie Patrick

Silhouette Romance

Wedding Bells and Diaper Pins #1095
The Marriage Chase #1130
Three Kids and a Cowboy #1235
Boot Scootin' Secret Baby #1289
The Millionaire's Proposition #1413
His, Hers...Ours? #1467

NATALIE PATRICK

believes in romance and has firsthand experience to back up that belief. She met her husband in January and married him in April of that same year—they would have eloped sooner, but friends persuaded them to have a real wedding. Ten years and two children later, she knows she's found her real romantic hero.

Amid the clutter in her work space, she swears that her headstone will probably read, "She left this world a brighter place but not necessarily a cleaner one." She certainly hopes her books brighten her readers' days.

IT'S OUR 20th ANNIVERSARY!
We'll be celebrating all year,
Continuing with these fabulous titles,
On sale in August 2000.

Intimate Moments

#1021 A Game of Chance
Linda Howard

#1022 Undercover Bride
Kylie Brant

#1023 Blade's Lady
Fiona Brand

SECRETS! **#1024 Gabriel's Honor**
Barbara McCauley

#1025 The Lawman and the Lady
Pat Warren

#1026 Shotgun Bride
Leann Harris

Special Edition

#1339 When Baby Was Born
Jodi O'Donnell

#1340 In Search of Dreams
Ginna Gray

#1341 When Love Walks In
Suzanne Carey

#1342 Because of the Twins...
Carole Halston

#1343 Texas Royalty
Jean Brashear

#1344 Lost-and-Found Groom
Patricia McLinn

Desire

 #1309 The Return of Adams Cade
BJ James

 #1310 Tallchief: The Homecoming
Cait London

 #1311 Bride of Fortune
Leanne Banks

 #1312 The Last Santini Virgin
Maureen Child

 #1313 In Name Only
Peggy Moreland

#1314 One Snowbound Weekend...
Christy Lockhart

Romance

#1462 Those Matchmaking Babies
Marie Ferrarella

 #1463 Cherish the Boss
Judy Christenberry

#1464 First Time, Forever
Cara Colter

 #1465 The Prince's Bride-To-Be
Valerie Parv

#1466 In Want of a Wife
Arlene James

#1467 His, Hers...Ours?
Natalie Patrick

Prologue

"The princess looked like a goner for sure."

Wayne Perry hung back in the doorway of the nursery, where the baby-sitter was putting Clark and Becky Winstead's two-year-old twin daughters to bed. Though he couldn't remember a time when he hadn't known Becky, who was his law partner's little sister, he had only met Clark on social occasions. Those came few and far between in Wayne's tiny hometown of Woodbridge, Indiana. It felt strange to be in the man's posh home in the Chicago suburbs with both Clark and Becky out for the evening. But Wayne had not come to see the Winsteads. He'd come to see *her*.

"But that plucky princess knew something her adversary didn't—she knew she had everything she needed to take care of herself."

Wayne paused for a moment to indulge in the

sight and sound of the young woman, letting her words fade from his conscious mind. Despite her reputation as a hard-driven drone with a queen-bee attitude, Shelley Harriman, Clark Winstead's right-hand "man," seemed quite at home in the large rocker between two pink-and-white cribs. She looked younger than he expected and prettier, much prettier.

At first Wayne had resisted his partner's request that he work with Clark's administrative assistant. Then the anniversary party he'd volunteered to host for the Taylors and Winsteads began to grow. Before he could book the Woodbridge VFW Hall and hire a band, the event had taken on a life of its own, including the element of keeping the whole thing a surprise from the wives. That level of sneakiness, he'd decided, required a woman's touch.

"She struggled to lift the mighty blade."

Not that Wayne distrusted women or disliked them. Quite the opposite; he just had a healthy respect for their abilities and frailties. He made another quick once-over of the woman with the rich-brown hair tumbling in sexy disarray from the tightly wound bun high on her head. Shelley, Clark had informed him, had plenty of both.

Looking at her now, Wayne had to question how well the man really knew the woman who virtually ran his office. Clark had spoken of her as he might a computer or fax machine, giving a matter-of-fact description of her strengths and weaknesses as they applied to the jobs Wayne might ask her to perform. But Shelley was no machine. He understood that almost intuitively as he watched the light in her eyes shift when she went from weaving her animated tale to gazing with tender concern at the babies in her charge.

"She wondered if she had taken on too much, if she was worthy of the task before her. Could she do it? Or would she fail and lose everything?" Shelley's slender fingers gripped the edge of the big red book propped on her lap. Her expression conveyed total empathy with the plight of the fictitious princess. She paused, wet her lips, then sniffed and jerked her shoulders straight.

Those unguarded gestures got to Wayne in ways that hours of getting-to-know-you chitchat never could. Though this was the first time he'd ever laid eyes on Shelley, he could see right into her heart. Shelley was the princess in her story.

"But what could the princess do? There was no one else to face down the dreaded beast but her."

"That's what you think," Wayne muttered under his breath. He might not be the workaholic that his law partner Matt Taylor was and he doubted that he'd ever be as rich as Shelley's boss, Clark Winstead, but there was one thing Wayne knew how to do and do well. Wayne was a lifelong rescuer of ladies in distress.

"So the princess drew upon all the strength she had within her, seized the sword lying at her feet and thrust it high." Shelley's hand shot up.

Wayne raised his own fist in triumph from the safety of the shadows.

"With fiery determination she fought back the ferocious dragon, blow by blow, inch by inch until…" Holding the storybook open on her lap, she rose out of the chair just enough to check on each twin.

For one fleeting instant, longing for things that could never be swelled inside him before he pushed that down and reason returned. Could he blame the cozy atmosphere of the nursery? The comforting glow of the single lamp on its lowest setting? Or the smell of small children bathed and powdered and snuggled in bed? Something deep within him knew those alone could not have stirred such sincere, unrestrained emotion in a man like him. Shelley Harriman had touched his heart. She got to him because he knew she was the one thing he had vowed he would never get involved with again—a woman who needed him.

A flutter of flannel blanket in one crib sent Shelley back into the seat and to the story. "Until at last, the dragon, seeing it could not coerce, control, or consume her, threw up his scaly dragon claws in surrender. And he and the princess made an appointment to meet again at her office and draw up the proper papers for their peaceful coexistence." She closed the book, which she had not looked at once as she'd sat spinning her colorful tale for the two toddlers now fast asleep. Standing, she peered into one crib and caressed a head of blond curls.

Then she turned to the next child, dropped a brief kiss on a chubby pink cheek and murmured, "And they lived happily ever after."

"You left out the part where the knight in shining armor charges in to rescue the fair maiden."

She whipped her head around. Her body tensed. Eyes narrowed, she looked ready to do to Wayne or any intruder what the princess in her story had done to the dragon, and worse.

Since he had no intention of being filleted at swordpoint or of signing papers stripping him of his...dragonhood, he did something he knew would nip that nonsense right in the bud. He smiled.

Her jaw went slack. Literally slack.

He chuckled, then gave her an obvious, slow once-over before saying, "Now about that knight in shining armor—"

"This is a modern fairy tale, where the heroine is quite capable of rescuing herself, thank you very much." She tipped her head up enough to give the impression of looking down her nose at him, even though she stood a good five inches too short to actually do that. Still, the way she clutched the book to her chest made her look endearingly vulnerable and unsure.

"Sometimes, even in modern days, fair maidens get themselves into fixes that require—" he stepped close enough to tug the book from her grasp, glanced down at it, then fixed his eyes intently on hers "—knightly intervention."

She gave the sweetest, almost imperceptible gasp at his double entendre but did not let it rattle her. "Mr. Perry, I presume?"

"Miss Harriman." He stuck out his right hand while he held the large storybook by the spine with his left.

Only a moment of hesitation welcomed his handshake when she put her hand in his. Her cool fingers betrayed the slightest tremble, then she gripped his hand and gave a firm shake, like a general taking command of the troops. "Thank you for coming to Chicago to meet with me tonight."

"Thank you for agreeing to pitch in on this project." He returned her shake in kind, then to reassure her that her rescuer had arrived, continued to hold her hand gently in his. "I appreciate the backup you're giving me. Obviously there are some things that can't get done in a town the size of Woodbridge."

"Just as there are some things I can't do in Chicago for a party staged in Indiana."

They stood, gazes locked, in the dimness of the nursery. Neither showed any sign of surrendering control until one of the babies fussed. Shelley's hard facade fell away, replaced by the soft expression of concern he had first seen. She tiptoed to the cribs to make a quick check of the children, and one of them tossed and kicked, then quieted. She watched and waited, then sighed audibly and turned toward him.

He extended his hand toward the hallway, silently suggesting they take the discussion else-where.

She pushed ahead of him, leading the way through the hallway that took them toward the front of the house.

He was the first to speak. "Matt gave me a broad overview of what he'd like to see done."

"Mr. Winstead drew up explicit instructions for the party as he envisions it."

Their feet hardly made a sound in the long dark hallway. The air between them had a brittle quality that practically crackled and popped like electric-ity. That was not the result of their shoes skimming the thick soft carpet.

Wayne found Shelley's anxiety over the simple party plans sweet. She wanted to please her boss, wanted to do a good job, wanted it so badly she let fear of failing motivate her choices and actions. The valiant effort over something so small spoke to Wayne. This was just the tip of the iceberg and he knew it.

His old instinct to climb into the pilot's seat and protect another vulnerable woman sparked again. Even though he'd sworn off those ways years ago and it was the last thing he needed in his life, he could clearly see it was the one thing Shelley needed. It was just a party, after all, not saving her from a manipulative man or from a self-destructive life-style. And if, with his help and guidance, she came a little closer to being the princess who could take up her own sword, all the better. As they entered the two-story foyer, he opened his mouth to tell her as much.

"Mr. Perry, I think before we can work together to create a beautiful and memorable party for your friends and my employer, there is one thing we have to get straight."

"I couldn't agree more."

"There are a thousand tiny details that must be ironed out, organized and carried through."

"Well, a thousand might be carrying it a bit too far."

She shut her eyes and shook her head. "That attitude is at the root of the difficulty I already foresee us having, Mr. Perry."

"Glad you see it, too, Miss Harriman."

"I do. That's why I want us to reach an understanding before things go any further—"

"Don't worry, you can rest assured because—"

"I am in charge." They said the words in perfect unison.

Why did he suspect, Wayne thought as he met Shelley's unyielding gaze with one of his own, that was the last time they would stand united in anything for a very long time to come?

Chapter One

Five weeks later

"Let's get straight to the bottom line, Wayne. It's time to set a date and go forward with these wedding plans."

Perfect! Shelley congratulated herself on the cool detached delivery of her well-rehearsed message. No hysteria. No distress. Not so much as a hint of accusation in her tone.

Now if she could do it just like that when she actually had that infuriating Wayne Don't-worry-your-pretty-little-head Perry on the other end of the line. She loosened her grip on the silent telephone receiver and fit it back into its cradle with a decisive click. She crossed her arms low over her midsection, as if that might quiet the fluttering there.

She would call. Any minute now she would pick up that phone, punch the number for an outside line, dial up the law firm of Taylor and Perry in Woodbridge, Indiana, and say her piece.

She'd do it, she told herself, after she collected her thoughts. She'd get up her nerve, take a deep breath and do the one thing she found most difficult in the world—risk making a complete idiot of herself in front of a man. In this case, a successful, well-spoken man with the kind of dazzling blue eyes that made a girl sigh before she even realized she had.

Shelley's shoulders rose and fell as she let out a soft breath. Mr. Winstead, her boss, liked to joke that if he looked up the word "efficient" in the dictionary, he'd find a picture of Shelley. Well, if that same dictionary had a listing for the precise antonym for her, it would give one name: Wayne Perry.

Friendly and forthright, that man didn't give a rip what people thought of him. Yet she'd bet her bottom dollar—if she was the sort foolish enough to squander money in a wager—that everyone he met thought well of him. Well, almost everyone.

Laid-back, people called him with jovial admiration. "He doesn't sweat the small stuff," they said.

"But the devil is in the details," Shelley muttered. Devilishness, she suspected Mr. Perry understood tenfold, but details? She'd seen nothing of those in the flurry of e-mails, phone calls and disastrous meetings they'd had over the past month trying to coordinate the simplest of plans.

A surprise wedding! Shelley reached up to twist a strand of deep-brown hair that had worked loose from her tight topknot. The very idea of weddings made her anxious enough, but to do it for people she hardly knew? How had she gotten stuck arranging everything from gowns to getaways without letting the bride in on it until the very day of the ceremony?

Brides, plural, she thought, making a quick mental correction. As if the whole secret ceremony scenario wasn't enough, she had to do it in duplicate to accommodate her boss's brother-in-law. He also wanted to give his wife the wedding their hasty courthouse marriage had supplanted six years ago. And so Wayne Perry came into the picture.

As Matthew Taylor's law partner and best friend, Wayne seemed the most likely candidate to assist with the preparations. Shelley had assured her boss that she could handle everything, of course. She had not needed to remind him that she had never let him down before on any assignment large or small. She would have convinced him, too, if they had not decided to hold the services in Indiana. With that one decision, the participation of that cocky, arrogant, thinks-he-knows-everything and has-to-be-in-charge-of-it-*all* man became a necessity.

She scanned her silent, neutral-toned office. It looked much as it had the day she'd accepted this job five years ago. Except now the desk gleamed with a hand-rubbed polish. Silk plants replaced the unpredictable live ones that had sat by the windows like leafy green time bombs, ready to turn brown, droop or dry up at any moment.

Wayne Perry's office, no doubt, buzzed with music, conversation and laughter. She could just imagine the chaos and clutter of family photos on desks, knickknacks on the credenza, maybe a spare tie tossed over the back of a chair. And probably a dying ficus in the corner shedding leaves on the carpet like confetti at a New Year's Eve extravaganza. That was the kind of man she was dealing with here.

The kind of man, she feared, who'd consider an accident-prone, twenty-five-year-old, career-focused little drudge like her the perfect foil for his gentle, humorous, good-natured self. She knew that kind of man all too well. She'd almost married the original Mr. Laugh-and-the-whole-world-laughs-with-you. Or in Shelley's case, laughs at you.

Memories of old hurts and embarrassments came flooding back. Daddy, trying to raise three children alone after her mother died, had often warned Shelley never to trust a man because they only wanted one thing. To that, her brothers had taunted, "Shelley, you don't have to worry—men may only want one thing, but you ain't got what they want."

Before she could catch herself, her thoughts

flashed back to the one time she had tried to prove both her brothers and her father wrong. She'd finally thought she'd found the one man who could love her body *and* her mind. Four years ago she'd started dating the boy next door, Ron Fuller. She didn't think she loved him, but everyone told her she did. She didn't think she was ready to marry him, but he insisted she was. She didn't listen to her heart. She let outside pressure from her father and brothers and most of all, Ron, guide her decisions.

Her cheeks grew hot and her chest felt tight just thinking of how she'd last seen her ex-fiancé on the day they were supposed to get married. She could still remember the excuses she'd made for him being late for the small ceremony in her family's backyard. Still hear the swish-swish-swish of her hand-sewn wedding gown as she marched to look for him in the house next door. Still feel all the eyes filled with pity as the entire wedding party watched her walk in on Ron with another woman.

Just barely a woman, to be precise, in age and maturity. But undoubtedly more a woman than Shelley had been in the ways that seemed to matter to Ron.

Shelley was wiser now, of course. That wisdom, though, had come with a price. Now she had to stay on her toes at all times, guard against being made a fool of by anyone of the opposite sex. She had lost her ability to trust a man.

Her experience with Ron had stripped her of

what little dignity and self-esteem she had left after a lifetime of being told she would not measure up as anything but a housekeeper, an assistant, a drone. Some good had come of it all, though. She had begun that day her fateful journey to total self-reliance. No one—more to the point, no man—would ever make her decisions for her or tell her what to do. She made her own way in life, lonely as that sometimes was. She had worked hard to rebuild what she could of her pride and to find some measure of self-worth in her work and accomplishments. She would never relinquish those feelings to anyone again.

So if there was any other way to tackle her job without involving Wayne Perry, she'd certainly do it. But she *had* to call him. She had to rely on his help. Without his help, she couldn't possibly arrange the detailed wedding her boss wanted as an anniversary present for his wife.

Planning a wedding. It made her sick just to think of it. Add to that the fact that the happy-go-lucky lawyer had canceled or cut short every conversation and meeting they'd had about this. That did nothing to quiet her nerves.

Okay, here goes. How could she criticize Perry for procrastinating while doing such a bang-up job of it herself? She twirled her finger until the lock of hair wrapped around it bit into her knuckle. She stole a sidelong glance at the black business phone sitting at the ready on her large tidy desk. *Perhaps just one more rehearsal—*

Chirrrp.

Shelley practically leaped out of her skin at the sound of the sedate electronic ring.

Chirrrp

She blinked, forcing away the uncharacteristic fogginess that this business with Wayne Perry had evoked in her. She jerked her chin up just an inch and smoothed back the stray hair. There, she felt pulled together, polished, untouchable.

"Winstead Corporation, International Headquarters. Clark Winstead's office, Miss Harriman speaking. What may I do for you?"

"What may you do for me, Miss Harriman? Or what do you do *to* me with that sexy voice of yours and that aloof unattainable act?"

"Hello, Mr. Davis." Baxter Davis, her boss's accountant and closest friend, got quite a charge out of his little game of flirting with her. Trying to get her to let her hair down, as he put it. One day, she felt sorely tempted, she would do just that and call his bluff. One day when monkeys flew past the window of her top-floor Chicago office, that is.

"Hello yourself, Shelley. I guess you know what I'm calling about."

"Mr. Winstead has left all the information you'll need to run the office while I'm working on the last-minute details for his party this week. I have everything in my files and can have it all sent over to your office immediately." She swiveled around in her chair.

"Gee, I'd hate to put you to any trouble."

"No trouble at all." If you don't count becoming a contortionist as trouble, she thought. With a tilt of her head, she trapped the receiver against her shoulder, leaving her hands free to pull open the file drawer. "If you don't want me to courier it over to you, you can have your assistant come to my office. I'll have everything ready."

"I'd rather come by myself. Been a while since I saw that pretty face of yours. I don't suppose you're wearing your hair down today, are you, Miss Harriman?"

"My hair is..." Her gaze flicked upward. She scowled at her reflection in the huge gilt-framed mirror hanging above the credenza behind her desk. Today she had not the usual one, but two pencils poked in her hair. One was stabbed into the compact little bun on top of her head, and the other poked out from behind her right ear. The second one had caused that tendril of dark wavy hair to fall alongside her neck and lie in a lazy *S* against the collar of her off-white blouse.

She made a note to fix that before she called Wayne Perry. He'd never know how disheveled she looked, but she would know, and it might show in her tone or demeanor.

"My hair is hardly relevant to this discussion, Mr. Davis. The files will be ready whenever you need them."

"Fine. Play it that way." The hum of the dial tone stopped her from saying more.

"Nice talking to you, too," she muttered, still holding the receiver under her chin.

She continued to rummage through the files. For an instant she thought of hanging up. But since the interruption would mean starting all over in her search, having to paw through the packed files to find the one she had not yet begun to wriggle free, she decided against it. Besides, as long as she had the phone off the hook, she might as well get in that one last rehearsal for her big call.

She bent down, rising out of her chair. Her fingers strained to give her the added centimeters she needed to pluck out the color-coded file from the back of the credenza drawer. She gritted her teeth and channeled her frustration into her practice phone call.

"Wayne Perry..." She almost had the file in her fingertips.

Her chair creaked.

Despite the twinge in her shoulders, she stretched just a smidgen more. She went on tiptoe, lifting her backside higher. That should give her just enough extra oomph to snag that file.

Another creak that did not quite register as the chair's complaining scraped at her raw nerves and set her teeth on edge. With a deep breath, she let the full weight of her irritation spur on her reach and fire up her memorized lines. "Wayne Perry, let's get straight to the bottom line!"

"And such a lovely bottom line it is!"

She knew that voice and it did not belong to

Baxter Davis. Shelley froze. Just like that, head in a drawer, arms in a lurch, rear end high in the air. Lovely, indeed!

"If I'd only known this is where you wanted to begin things, Miss Harriman, I'd have made the trip from Woodbridge weeks ago."

She thought of bolting upright. One fast spin around and she could skewer the man with the withering glare that had earned her the office nickname "Ol' Sour Glower." For absolutely any other human being she would have done it.

She lifted her head just enough to peer into the mirror.

Wayne Perry smiled at her.

Her jaw dropped.

His gaze took an appreciative dip.

She could practically feel it sliding over the curve of her behind, down her long legs, then up again. Slowly. She shivered.

He fixed his gaze on hers, a blue-eyed gaze the likes of which she'd never seen this side of Paul Newman in a late-night movie on her thirteen-inch TV.

Shelley sighed.

"Hi."

She murmured something even she couldn't understand.

"I know I took a chance just showing up like this. But I had the time and figured, what the heck, why not shoot up to Chicago and see how the wedding plans are going. Bad timing?"

"No, not at all. I was just trying to get my hands on some eyes."

He frowned, just slightly.

Shelley straightened. The forgotten receiver tucked between chin and shoulder fell into the file drawer, creating a *ka-thunk* worthy of the sound a drummer makes after a bad joke. "*Files.* I was trying to get my hands on some files."

"Looks like you did it." He nodded to the folders she had pressed to her chest.

"Yes. I promised someone I'd have these ready to pick up and *I* always do what I say I will."

"Ouch." His smile told her he understood that veiled indictment of his lax attitude in the wedding-planning department.

She lifted her chin. Cool and detached, she reminded herself. She sat down and rotated her chair in the proper direction. "What a coincidence your showing up here so unexpectedly, Mr. Perry. I was just planning to call you."

"Planning to?" He flicked open the buttons on his dark-blue suit jacket.

Shelley swallowed hard. She couldn't help noticing the flatness of the man's abdomen beneath the smooth cloth of his shirt and how graceful yet strong his long fingers were.

"You were just *planning* to call me, Miss Harriman?" He tipped his head and a lock of hair tumbled carelessly forward. His voice carried no trace of sarcasm or censure. His eyes glittered with an invitation for her to join him in the humor of the situation. "From what I just heard, it sounded to me like you were already reading me the riot act."

"Oh." She pursed her lips. Her cheeks grew hot. "Oh, that. It was...I just...just a little bit of preplanning on my part so that everything would go smoothly once—"

"Excuse me, but did you say *pre*planning?"

"Yes."

"And preplanning is different from regular planning because...?"

"Because it's a different stage of the process. You can't just jump into planning all willy-nilly, Mr. Perry."

"No, of course not." Somehow he infused his obviously teasing remark with empathy.

Shelley knew he was mocking her, but she did not *feel* he was mocking her. In fact, she felt—

"Willy-nilly," he repeated softly.

Exactly, she thought.

He whisked one hand down his tie, which had seemed quite conservative until he moved toward her desk. "I've been accused of a lot of things in my life..."

"No doubt." She tipped her head to confirm that she saw the cartoon characters hidden among the small paisley print.

He chuckled, a quick gentle sound, yet decidedly masculine. "As I was saying, I've been accused of a lot of things in my life, but willy-nillyism is not one of them."

The intimate rumble in his voice left her speechless.

He moved closer and closer until just the corner of the desk jutted between them.

She could feel his presence, a force somehow bigger than his physical body, which was nothing trifling to begin with. Her gaze latched on to his. She could not help it. She wanted to look away, but the power and emotional energy in those eyes held her fast.

"You know something, Miss Harriman?"

"What?"

He sat on the desk corner, then angled his body until his face was just inches from hers. "I think you and I working together is going to prove very interesting."

So did she. But unlike him, she could also see the danger lurking beneath that...interest. He had already caught her at a disadvantage once. She would not give him any further latitude by letting him see how his nearness affected her.

"I think working together will be just that, Mr. Perry. Work." Without so much as a cursory glance, she reached back to the open file drawer. Business as usual.

"Miss Harriman, maybe you should..." Wayne pointed toward the credenza.

Shelley raised her chin. She gave the drawer a shove. Its metal casters clattered quietly. "No one tells me how to do my job, Mr. Perry. No one ever needs to. I assure you I am the consummate professional in everything I undertake.''

Just then the springy cord that connected the receiver to the phone went taut. The file drawer banged shut. The telephone jerked off her desk and crashed to the floor.

He did not laugh out loud. If she'd been in a more generous frame of mind, she'd have given him some credit for that small kindness. She glared at him and bent to retrieve the phone.

He bent over at the same time she did.

She grabbed the phone just as his large fingers wrapped around it, trapping her hands beneath his grasp.

The closeness of their bodies in the small space charged the air with a new sense of intimacy.

''I can take care of this by myself, thank you.'' She tugged at the phone. The sudden movement dragged him toward her, but he did not let go.

''Sometimes it's nice to have someone to lend a little comfort and aid. Everyone longs for that from time to time. Even you, Miss Harriman.''

Had she been a more worldly woman, she truly believed the man would have kissed her right then and there. Or maybe she would have kissed him. He was the kind of man, she knew instinctively, who kissed women in a moment of passionate impulse. Or inspired women to kiss him. To which he would offer no resistance, she could well imagine.

She wasn't widely experienced, but she did have

enough of an education with that kind of man to know she wanted nothing to do with one. She yanked the phone away and stood in one fluid movement. "I don't need any man to lend me comfort and aid, Mr. Perry."

One, the twenty-four-hour-a-day instant critic in her brain amended. She did not need any*one* to lend her comfort and aid. Luckily the split second it took her to berate herself for that mistake prevented her from blurting out that she did not need a man for anything because she could take care of everything all by herself. Oh, the fun he could have at her expense over that. Or worse, the pity he might feel.

"I am first, last and always a strong, capable professional, Mr. Perry." The jarring impact of her slamming the phone on the desk produced a quiet *clang.*

"I don't doubt that for one moment." He gave her a nod, then his lips curved in a hint of a smile. "That doesn't mean—"

She held up her hand to cut him off. "It means we have to make some ground rules. First one being that in the future you should call before you come to see me."

"I apologize about that, but you see—"

"Apology accepted." This was more like it. She had regained the upper hand. She could now move forward with confidence and be in control. She turned to pluck the phone receiver out of the drawer, acting as if it was so routine it appeared on her job description. "This is my place of work, Mr. Perry, and I will accept nothing short of absolute professional decorum here at all times."

"Where's Mistress of Office Misbehavior? The Dominatrix of Data-Handling Disobedience? Baxter's here and he's been a very naughty boy!"

"Professional decorum, eh?" Wayne's eyes sparkled with undisguised delight.

Shelley wanted to strangle Baxter, who'd sauntered in smiling like the proverbial Cheshire cat. Or maybe she could just crawl into the open file drawer and lock herself in there until after the wedding date was long past.

The weddings. She had a job to do. "Mr. Perry, I—"

"Look, obviously, I've caught you at a bad time, Miss Harriman." The lean lawyer checked his watch. "How about if I come back in half an hour and we go to lunch? We have a lot to get done in a short time."

She'd been going to say that.

"I'll see you then." He gave Baxter a nod, then strode for the office door.

Shelley wet her lips, wanting to call out after him, to have the last word and reestablish who was in charge. Before she got a sound out, he turned just enough to keep his straight back and broad shoulders in view. Her breath caught in her throat.

"I think I'm going to like working with you, comfort and aid not withstanding, *Mistress Harriman*."

The door swung shut behind him.

Shelley's pulse pounded. She clenched her teeth, and in a display of utmost professional comportment, she let out a mild curse and kicked the file drawer closed.

Chapter Two

"Who is that Baxter jerk and what gives him the right to speak to Shelley that way?"

"I dunno." The young man who'd let Wayne sit at his table in the crowded coffee shop on the ground floor of the building shrugged.

"None of my business, of course. That's why I took off and allowed them some privacy." Wayne tapped his stir stick on the edge of his cappuccino cup. "None of my damn business who she sees. Or who calls her Dominatrix of Disobedience."

"Whoa. Cool."

Wayne checked his watch. What he saw was the image of Shelley up in that glass-and-flash box of an office with that creep leering at her. As a man fresh from a little recreational leering himself, he resented anyone else horning in on the pleasure. "I ought to march right back up there and toss the bum out.''

''Could be trouble. You must really care about this chick.''

''Actually I hardly know her.''

''She must be something, then.''

''She is something.'' He took a sip of the rich drink, then looked into his cup as the liquid burned its way down his throat. ''I just can't decide exactly what yet.''

''Then why let yourself get worked up over her and that Baxter dude?''

Wayne smiled. Most people who knew him would find themselves hard-pressed to imagine him worked up over anything. Around his hometown of Woodbridge, Indiana, his relaxed approach and ability to find the humor in almost anything made his law partner joke that they ought to amend the title on his office door to Wayne Perry, Attorney-at-ease.

Nothing, most people who knew that side of him would tell you, got under his skin. But anyone who truly believed that about him would be wrong.

Two things fired Wayne up. They sustained his dreams and ambitions. One was the fundamental need for honor and integrity. He demanded those of himself and expected them in the few people he trusted unequivocally. He'd learned younger than most that involvement with anyone lacking in those basic qualities was torment. He'd also learned that he would do anything to fight for and protect someone who risked losing touch with those qualities.

The other thing that moved and motivated Wayne was the exhilarating lure of the unknown, of discovery and conquest.

In Shelley Harriman, he saw potential for all of that and more. She was the kind of woman who could definitely get under his skin.

That was why he had to remain on his toes around her—and why he couldn't get her out of his head. Since their very first conversation, he'd felt a connection with her that had rattled, irritated, then intrigued him. Finally it led him to Chicago today for one reason and one reason alone. He'd come to dazzle Shelley Harriman.

Dazzle her. He would settle for nothing less concerning this woman. He wanted her to be as impressed with him as he was with her.

"It's beyond reason, I'll give you that, to get worked up over a woman with a personality as tightly wound as that bun she wears her hair in."

"The Dominatrix." The young man nodded wisely and stroked the scraggly red hairs on his chin.

"And the worst of it is, there's no future in it. Even if I were looking for a future with the woman, which I'm not."

"I hear you there, man."

"Shelley and I could never have more than the next week together. And then we have to stay strictly focused on the weddings."

''Did you say weddings?''

''Still, when a man finds a woman who embodies the essence of the only things that fuel his inner fire, he has to do something to make a connection, even one that can't possibly last.''

''No, dude, I could swear you said weddings. That doesn't sound like someone planning to make a short-term hookup.''

''Yeah, don't get hung up on that part. See, her boss had this idea, and she and I got roped into planning— Actually she called it preplanning. Isn't that great? Preplanning?'' He shook his head. Every time he crossed paths with Shelley, he found something else compelling about her.

Something in her eyes warmed him. Something in her ideas intrigued him. Something in her voice, strong yet vulnerable, brought out his urge to defend her and, yes, to dazzle her, both at once.

And while he hung around some unfamiliar coffee shop to do that, some greasy-haired guy named Baxter had her alone in that office. Wayne got up from the table and headed for the door.

''Whoa, where you going, dude? You said you couldn't go back up there for half an hour.''

''So I'm early. Let me give you a piece of advice, kid.''

''Sure. I'm not going anywhere.''

''There are times with women when you can really use all that politically correct crap about being sensitive to your advantage. You know, play it up right, let your guard down a little. Women eat that up. For about this long." He snapped his fingers.

The younger man blinked, his head barely nodding.

"But deep down, when all's said and done, women still want a man of action. And deep down, that's the kind of guy I am."

"Gotta be true to yourself, man."

"You got it." Wayne hit the door, muttering under his breath as he pounded into the building's marble lobby. "I gotta be me, Shelley's gotta be Shelley, and Baxter's gotta hit the road."

Go! Get out! Take a hike! That's what she wanted to say. Instead, she swiveled her chair toward the computer screen, closed a file with a quiet double click and said, "That's everything Mr. Winstead wanted you to have, Mr. Davis. I'm sure you'll find it's all in order."

"That's the way it always is with you, isn't it, Miss Harriman?" Baxter leaned in so that he was practically draped over her desk. "Everything in order? Don't you ever long to do something wild and crazy?"

Wild and crazy? she thought. Like what? Push her boss's best friend off her desk, then run to the door and scream for someone to come save her from his boorish behavior?

"If that's all, Mr. Davis, there are a few things I need to tend to before my luncheon engagement."

"Ah. Lunch. With that blond guy with the—" he slashed his hand a few inches over his head to indicate Wayne's height, then puffed out his chest and flexed his arms in a parody of the other man's brawn "—overblown ego?"

"Said the kettle about the pot," she muttered under her breath.

"Come on, Shelley, don't tell me you wouldn't rather have lunch with someone like me."

"No, I wouldn't." And she meant it. Heaven help her, she was actually looking forward to her lunch with the man who'd been fouling up her well-laid plans for weeks. "Um, if you'll excuse me, I think I'll just freshen up before—"

"Going to let your hair down for *him?*"

If she'd been a man, she'd have decked him. That was how sleazy he made the simple phrase sound. She turned her back on Baxter without a word.

"Hey, just fooling around with you, Shelley. You know our little inside private joke?"

She peered into the mirror, feigning endless fascination with her collar, her buttons, her sleeve.

"You don't have to let your hair down to make yourself beautiful for any man, you know that, don't you?" Baxter came up behind her.

She tensed.

"No, you never have to take your hair down, but maybe you should take the pencils out of it." He tugged one free.

"Oh." She took it, feeling silly and, oddly,

nothing else. When Wayne Perry had stood this close to her, she'd been one quivering mass of sensations, thoughts and emotions. "Thank you."

"Here, let me get the other one."

"No, please. I can get it myself."

"It's no problem, really."

The metal band of the pencil snagged her hair. "Ow!"

"If you wouldn't fight me, this would be much easier."

"Stop. Please, I don't want you to—"

"Hold still and just let me—"

"The lady told you to stop."

"Wayne?" Shelley whipped her head around just as Wayne yanked Baxter backward. The pencil tore loose from her bun, taking a few strands of hair with it. "What do you think you're...?"

He didn't hit Baxter, but then, he didn't have to. Wayne's presence alone sent the other man scurrying.

"Your pencil." Baxter handed it to her, collected the files he'd originally come for, then hightailed it out of there.

Shelley clenched her teeth. Wayne Perry accomplished more boundary setting with Baxter by just entering the room than she had managed with volumes of tightly worded, carefully controlled requests and diversions. Why didn't she feel more appreciative of that?

Because Wayne had made her feel foolish, that's why. He'd made her feel like some pathetic female who had such limited experience with men that even the slightest hint of seduction would prove too much for her to cope with. He'd made her feel inadequate and stolen her sense of control—however wobbly—out of her hands. That was one thing she accepted from no man.

"Good thing I came back when I did."

"Oh, puh-leeze! Save your macho posturing for someplace where it might count for something. Perhaps there's a rodeo in town in need of a clown...or some premium, first-class bull."

He laughed. "I like you, Shelley Harriman. I really like you."

"Well, thank you. Your kind words will come in handy should I ever have to make an acceptance speech for an Oscar." She turned her back to him. Looking in the mirror, she tried to tuck a few loose tresses back into her topknot.

"You do that. In the meantime, why not cut a guy some slack? I was just trying to—"

"I know, lend me comfort and aid." She only made her hairstyle worse by fiddling with it, but she would not give up. "As I told you before, Mr. Perry, I don't need a man to give me those things."

"Too bad, because like it or not I've already come to your aid." He swept his hand upward from the base of her neck while the other slid a hairpin from her bun. "And as for comfort..."

She swallowed hard.

He inched closer.

She stiffened.

He pinned the stray strands neatly in place and whispered, "Well, I think we both might have enjoyed a little of that."

She had to get rid of this man. Shelley kept up a clipped pace leading the way to her usual table in the clean, quiet diner where she ate lunch daily. Wayne's style and hers were entirely too conflicted. He had to go.

It would be easy enough to accomplish. They'd simply review the list of wedding preparations and divvy them up. Things that could be accomplished from Chicago—picking up gowns, checking travel arrangements and so forth—she could handle quite easily alone. Things that required the Woodbridge connection, double-checking to make sure they had the church, the hall, the food and flowers, fell to him. That shouldn't take more than the lunch hour to clarify. Then goodbye, Mr. Perry, until just before the ceremonies.

She indicated her familiar table with a wave of her hand.

Wayne pulled out a chair for her.

She took the other seat. "So, I have what I consider a very comprehensive checklist of preparations that can be divided—"

He plucked the yellow legal pad from her hands and set it on the edge of another nearby table for two. "I thought we came here to eat."

She snatched back the pad, the paper ruffling. "Haven't you ever heard of a working lunch?"

"Why, shucks no, Miss Harriman. You and your big-city ways are a pure puzzlement to a poor old hayseed like me." With every overplayed word he edged his chair farther beneath the table until his legs touched hers.

She gasped and scooted backward.

His eyes glinted with amusement.

"No offense intended, Mr. Perry." She laced her arms over the legal pad and hugged it to her chest.

"No offense taken, Miss Harriman." He pinched one corner of the legal pad with his thumb and fore-finger and gave it a tug. "But I'm the kind of man who keeps his business and his pleasure separate."

The pad went sliding from her grasp.

He glanced up and with just a look succeeded in summoning the waitress.

Shelley sat in silent marvel. Despite years as a regular customer, it still took her several rounds of throat clearing and watch checking to get that same woman to take her order.

"When I work, I work, and when I eat lunch, I eat lunch." He slapped the legal pad down with finality.

The waitress approached, pencil at the ready.

"And when I get around to making wedding plans—" he slid the laminated menu from its chrome pocket "—I make wedding plans like no-body's business."

Shelley blinked.

"Oh, Miss Harriman, you're planning your wedding!" Shelley never realized the waitress even knew her name.

But not only did the woman in the brown-and-gold uniform know it, she felt no compunction about serving Shelley's personal business up to the whole lunch crowd, along with a hearty helping of misinformation. "That is so sweet, Miss Harriman! I never even suspected you had a sweetheart. Now here you are getting married."

"Actually I'm—" Her voice came out barely above a murmur.

"And this must be your intended. My, but you are a handsome man, if I may say so."

"Hey, don't let me stop you." Wayne took the woman's hand in his just as pleasant as you please and glanced at her name tag. "Tammy."

Shelley scowled at him. A split-second shake of her head warned him not to egg the waitress on in her misconception.

Wayne just winked at Shelley and mouthed, "What's the harm?"

"What's the—" She cut herself off when her sharp tone made the waitress jump and turn to gape at her. She felt like crawling under the table. However, since that would only ruin a perfectly good pair of panty hose and finish off one now only slightly tarnished reputation, she decided against it.

She unrolled her silverware and placed the napkin in her lap. Then she did what she could to pull her self-respect out of the fire. "What's the special today, Tammy?"

A minute later the waitress had taken their orders and hurried off. The instant she moved out of earshot, Shelley nailed Mr. Don't-let-me-stop-you with her best heart-halting glare. If she put this man in his place now, she'd save them both a lot of trouble in the long run. "I'd ask you if you lost your mind, but so far you haven't shown any signs that you have one."

"Why?" Wayne unfurled his own napkin. "Because I didn't embarrass the nice lady by pointing out her mistake?"

Okay, he got points for that, she thought, but still... "What about me?"

"I didn't think *you* should embarrass her, either," he said with a quiet conviction that sparked genuine regret in Shelley for her tart sarcasm.

"I meant, what about the way you complicated things for me? You didn't think twice about me when you let her go on like that."

"Don't kid yourself. Just because I didn't come to the same conclusion you would have doesn't mean I didn't think it through." His casual demeanor had a no-nonsense edge. "You'd better understand that now if we hope to work together with any success at all."

No nonsense—*that* she could relate to. She crossed her arms, then her legs, and sat back. "And you'd better understand that I won't be made a fool of, Mr. Perry, and I won't let someone else make my decisions for me. Get that through your head, or we won't work together at all.''

"I never intended to make a fool of you, and I think you know that.''

She believed him. The clenched knot her arms had made over her chest relaxed a bit. Her leg began to jiggle, making her knee bump against the underside of the small table.

"However, if my actions shook you up a little and maybe that gave me a peek at the woman behind that secretary-made-of-steel exterior you put on…well, I won't apologize for that.'' The corner of his mouth twitched upward just a hint. "See, I've decided I kind of enjoy disconcerting you, Miss Harriman.''

Then he must be loving every minute of this. She squirmed in her seat.

"Creates a nice healthy color in your cheeks, brings out the green in your eyes and sparks a real fire in that amazing voice of yours.'' He started to tuck his napkin into his shirt collar.

She snatched the napkin from his hand and threw it at his lap. "Well, I don't enjoy being…disconcerted. Not by you or any man.''

"I see.'' He leaned his forearms on the edge of the table and laced his fingers together. He gazed at her as if no one else in the world existed. Not like a sexual predator, but then again, not like a Boy Scout, either. And he seemed, though it might have been a trick of the flickering fluorescent lights, ready to listen to whatever she had to say and not just so he could make a joke of it.

She didn't know how she knew that, but she did. He conveyed it all without ever saying a word.

Shelley suddenly felt very feminine, but for the first time she sensed it as power, not as weakness. She wet her lips. "You think I have an amazing voice?"

"Yes, I do." If he was lying, someone needed to put his name on a ballot to run for office, because he was darn good at it.

Her pulse went haywire. "Thank you."

"You're welcome."

"Still, it wasn't very nice of you to embarrass me like that." At least she had some shred of survival instinct intact. As long as that remained, she could not simply let the statement he'd made go unchallenged. "Because if there's one thing I don't like, it's to be embarrassed."

"Then I apologize. I just didn't think it was such a big deal."

"It was to me," she said softly. She didn't realize until his brow furrowed that she had not spoken clearly enough to make herself heard. She glanced away to let him know she would not repeat herself.

He sighed. "I didn't see why it would be important to correct a total stranger about thinking we're planning our own wedding, instead of making arrangements for our friends."

"Our..." *Wedding.* The word would not form

on her lips. It wasn't a word she'd had a positive experience with, nor a word she ever expected to get much use out of again, for that matter. So, if Wayne wanted to spend this lunch tossing the term around between them, Shelley thought maybe it wasn't the worst thing that had ever happened to her. In fact, it made her feel sort of warm and wistful, as if maybe...

"It's not like it means anything, you know," he went on. "Not like letting someone else believe it is going to force us into some kind of relationship."

"Well, *somebody* had to say it," she muttered, jolted out of her momentary dream state.

"What?"

"Never mind." She shook her head. "And that's not entirely true. If we don't correct the waitress's ideas about us, it does mean something."

"Oh?" Instead of the doubt she anticipated, he edged closer, intrigued.

Not letting it faze her, she folded her hands on top of the table. "Yes. It means that at some point I will have to come up with some explanation about why I never married the man that nosy waitress saw me making wedding plans with. Either that or I'll have to find a new place to eat my lunch every day."

He sat back with enough force to make his wooden chair creak. "You eat your lunch at the same place every day?"

"Not on Saturday or Sunday." She bristled at

his incredulous tone. "But Monday through Friday, yes, I do eat in the same place. I have for the last five years, apart from the occasional lunch at my desk or with Mr. Winstead on business."

"That's unbelievable."

"Why? The food is good, the prices reasonable and it's close to work."

"But what about trying new things? What about seeing new people? What about seeking out new experiences? Don't you ever crave those? Don't you long for some variety?"

She got the distinct feeling he was talking about more than food. "I have variety. It's not like I order the same thing every day, for heaven's sake."

"Oh, well, that's different." He smirked, picked up the empty water glass, inspected it, then set it down. "As long as you don't order the same thing every day."

"Of course not. Let's see, there's—" she placed a finger to her cheek to feign calling up a list from memory "—Meat Loaf Monday, Turkey Club Tuesday, White Fish Wednesday…"

"Toxic Tedium Thursday," he threw in.

"Fooled You Friday." She arched an eyebrow, then gave a smug little smile.

"Yes! That's it!" Wayne slammed his flattened palm to the table, making it wobble. The other patrons of the small diner turned to stare. "There she is!"

People stopped with forks halfway to their mouths to turn and gape at the pair of them.

Shelley put her hand to her throat. "There *who* is?"

"You. Shelley Harriman. I knew you were in there somewhere." He laughed the way men do when they've just won some kind of contest.

Shelley wasn't sure, but she suspected that if the waitress had brought them a basket of rolls, the man would have spiked one like a football. And all because she made a stupid joke and smiled.

A sense of forbidding welled up in her stomach. She did not understand this unpredictable man or, worse yet, the clash of emotions he stirred up in her. He did not respond to her cool, professional manner, except to take it as some kind of challenge, something for him to get around and overcome. That made him seem, to Shelley, like a very dangerous man.

Fortunately for her, her foresight in laying the needed groundwork would provide a welcome buffer between them. Preparedness and control would pay off yet again. She reached over to refer to her legal pad with thoughtful authority. "While I'll concede your desire not to work while we eat, the food won't arrive for a few minutes. Let's make use of our time to go over a few things."

"I'm with you so far."

"I've taken the liberty of making some assignments. That way, once we've finished our meal, I can dive into my responsibilities here while you scurry on back to Woodbridge to tackle—''

"Uh-uh.'' He shook his head.

"I beg your pardon?''

"I'm not going back to Woodbridge, Miss Harriman.'' Once more he took the legal pad from her. This time he tossed it over his shoulder. It landed with a smack on the floor behind him.

Shelley started to launch into a lecture about putting someone's eye out and looking before you leap and how that applied to throwing things, too.

Before a sound formed on her lips, Wayne smiled. Those eyes searched hers.

It literally stole her breath away.

"Nope. No way. For weeks now you've dogged me about these wedding plans.''

"Dogged is a bit strong, don't you think?'' She winced.

"Whatever you call it, you obviously worried that I lacked real commitment to carrying off a first-class celebration.''

"I wondered, not so much as worried,'' she lied, suddenly aware of how harsh he made her sound.

"Worried or wondered, you needn't have bothered with either, Miss Harriman.'' He leaned back in his chair. He folded his arms over his open jacket just above those flat abs she'd already admired. "Because, for one thing, I love a party, and when I throw one, I throw one that's talked about for a long time to come.''

"I don't doubt that for a moment.'' She felt

frumpy just imagining the kind of parties a man like this might have.

"And more importantly, I made a promise to my friend that I would do this. And I will do it well."

"That's all I want. That we do everything possible to make this event truly special for Mr. and Mrs. Winstead—and for your friends, too."

"Then I'll make a little promise to you, too, Miss Harriman. I'm in for the duration. Whether we've got to work in Chicago or Woodbridge to get things set up right. Whatever it takes. I'll be right beside you every step of the way."

Chapter Three

Shelley cleared a spot on the table, then slapped the legal pad down with a satisfying *whap*.

Wayne did not so much as blink. He just sat there, his gaze trained on her. He had that in common with everyone else in the diner.

Who cared if others stared or whispered about her actions? She wouldn't be bullied or beguiled into spending the next week in Wayne's constant company. Keeping her defenses up, appearing cool and collected while working on wedding plans with those eyes always on her? No, she simply would not have it. The strain would be too much.

"The faster we divvy up the chores on the list I've prepared, Mr. Perry, the sooner we can go our separate ways."

"Oh, I'm so sorry." Wayne edged his chair closer to hers.

"Sorry? Why?" She resisted the urge to inch her own chair back a few inches.

"I didn't realize. But then, I can't imagine a competent person like yourself having neglected something as simple as a hearing test, Miss Harriman."

"Wh-what?"

"Seems I could be wrong."

"Now those are words that might come back to haunt you." Shelley tapped her pen against the pad. "But let me assure you my hearing is perfect."

"Then why are you acting as if you never heard me say that I'll be with you every step of the way until the weddings? In fact, it'll be every waking moment."

"Every waking moment?" She swallowed hard.

"Uh-huh."

She took a deep breath, then began scribbling on the yellow paper.

Wayne stretched his neck to see what she'd written. Aloud he read, "'Reminder to self—spend more time asleep.'"

He laughed.

Shelley held back as long as she could, but the complete lack of antagonism in Wayne's expression got to her. She smiled—a little.

"You know, you really are one sharp cookie even if you do have something of a chip on your shoulder." He slid the pen from her hand.

"Oh?" No one had ever dared tell her that to

her face before. To her surprise, the directness was not as threatening as she would have supposed. A man that up-front about things seemed pretty unlikely to want to make a fool of her. "A chip? Really?"

"Yeah. A big chip. I'd say right about here." He touched her shoulder.

She lowered her gaze to his strong hand. Could he feel the pounding of her heart, which seemed to consume her entire body, beneath his warm fingertips?

"I'll bet a lot of men find that off-putting." He eased his hand upward until it cupped the curve of her neck.

"I, uh, wouldn't know about a lot of men, Mr. Perry." She wanted to pull away from him. No, she didn't, but she knew she had to soon.

"Trust me."

She practically jumped away from his touch. "Trust you? What's that supposed to mean?"

"It means, trust me to know that a lot of men are turned off by the idea of working with a strong capable woman with a…no-nonsense attitude." He held out her pen to her. "Not me, of course."

She snatched it away. "I'd come back with a witty rejoinder, but that might give the impression that I cared one way or another what turns you on…um, off."

His lips twitched and his eyes sparked with subdued amusement.

"If we could just focus our attention on these lists I've made, now..."

"You're a challenge, Shelley. Anyone ever tell you that?"

"Only Baxter Davis."

"Not the same." He shook his head. "A man like that doesn't understand a challenge, not as it relates to a woman of your quality, not like I do."

Here it comes, she thought, the big play where he tried to take advantage of her supposed naiveté. Followed, after her rebuff, by the cutting remark at her expense. She'd been through it so many times it didn't even faze her. "What makes you so special in the understanding-women-of-my-quality department, Mr. Perry?"

"Because I've known too many people sadly lacking in the things I've come to admire about you in this short time we've known each other."

"Admire? You? The only thing I've ever noticed you admiring about me is my...you know." She lowered her gaze.

"And it's a damn fine 'you know,' too." He cocked his head and gave an obvious perusal. "Worthy of any man's admiration."

Shelley shifted in her seat.

"However, that's not what I was talking about."

"I'll just bet."

"I was talking about your inner qualities. Commitment, loyalty, self-discipline."

"Those hardly seem like the kinds of things that would matter to a man who wears cartoon-character ties. A man who can't be pinned down to work on an important project until a week before the event takes place. Or one who lies to a waitress about our supposed wedding, leaving me to clear things up after he's long gone.''

"In other words, you think I'm working some kind of angle, right?"

"It's been done before."

"Not by me. I don't operate that way."

"I'd like to take your word for that, but—"

"You don't have to take my word for it, Shelley. I am going to spend the next week proving it to you."

The woman seemed to have nothing to say to that. If she were a cat, her claws might have come out. Instead, she just sat there, her soft full lips slightly parted.

"Can I take your silence as implied consent to my hanging around all week?"

"You most certainly cannot!"

"Why not?"

"Why not what?"

"Don't play games with me, Shelley. Why refuse my offer of help?" He always went straight to the heart of the matter, and this was the thing he wanted most to understand about Shelley Harriman. Why was she so cool toward him? What made her act the way she did, and how could he make some kind of connection with the woman beneath the stern exterior? He doubted he'd get much of anything out of her without a bit of goading and some well-timed tweaking of those stoic sensibilities.

"I didn't refuse your help. I understand that your input is needed to pull the weddings together—needed back in Woodbridge."

"Why don't you want me to stay here and help you?" Wayne caught the approach of the waitress from the corner of his eye and timed his next words to coincide with her arrival. "You seemed plenty hot for it when I walked into your office earlier."

Her cheeks went red. Her lips paled. She glared at him through eyes no wider than slits. "If we weren't in a public place, I might do something I'd regret right now."

"Oh, yeah? Like what?" He folded his arms. "Let that prissy old-maid secretary facade of yours slip a notch? Show a flash of fire from the passionate woman churning beneath the surface? Go ahead, Shelley. Do it. I'd like to see it. And I'm sure Tammy here won't mind if you let your hair down a little, will you, Tammy?"

She smiled down at him over the two steaming plates in her hands. "No, sir. We like to think of this as the kind of place where people can just be themselves."

"See, Shelley? Why don't you just be yourself? Do what you've been dying to do since you rehearsed talking to me on the phone—let me have it."

"I have no intention of doing any such thing. I am far too much of a...a..."

"Chicken?" Tammy thrust a platter under Shelley's nose.

Wayne made a note to be sure to tip the waitress extra for her impeccable timing. He doubted that Shelley would be so generous.

"Now you be careful, Miss Harriman." Tammy set the chicken breast and steamed-veggie platter before Shelley. "Don't you get any grease on those wedding plans of yours."

"Actually, Tammy," said Wayne, "I was only having a little fun with you. We're planning someone else's anniversary party here, not our wedding." Even as he spoke to the waitress his gaze found Shelley's.

"Aw, that's too bad." Tammy gave him a wink as if to say she didn't think it was too bad at all as she put his plate of meat loaf and mashed potatoes in front of him. "You two made such a cute couple. Ketchup?"

"No thanks."

Tammy slid one corner of the bill for the meal discreetly under the napkin holder. "Well, if you need anything, anything at all, just holler."

"I will, but I doubt if Miss Harriman would dare," he said.

Tammy laughed as she headed away.

Shelley sniffed and began poking at her food with her fork.

"Bet you wish that was me you were stabbing, huh?"

She said nothing.

"Hmm." He took a jab at the grayish meat loaf lying in a pool of tomato paste and bacon grease. "Bland and yet not for the faint of heart, huh?"

"Are you talking about the food or the company?" She popped a piece of summer squash into her mouth.

Wayne sighed. "Okay. I guess it wouldn't hurt to go over your 'to do' list while we eat. It's certainly not going to detract from the pleasure of this unique dining experience."

"Excellent." Shelley nabbed the legal pad, her perfect nose tipped up just enough to show her satisfaction at getting her way, but not enough to seem haughty. "As I said before, if we divide these tasks and tackle them individually, I think we will achieve the best results in the shortest amount of time."

"I forgot to add mule-headed tenacity to your inventory of attributes." He tossed his napkin on the table. "Read the list."

"All right. First we have to pick up the wedding gowns at the dressmaker. I've been working with them on that already, so that job should fall to me." The pen rasped against the paper as she checked the item off.

"As a man who has a healthy respect for the way a woman looks in her clothes, maybe I should have some input into—"

"Don't be silly."

"I wasn't being silly." He pushed his plate away with the food untouched. "I think that as someone who knows both of the women involved far better than you do, my opinion of the gowns would have some merit."

"Oh, please. Have you ever picked out a wedding gown? Do you understand about fabric and form?" She tipped her head to one side and attempted a sneer.

The fact that she had not the slightest success at pulling off the effect of smug contempt touched something in him. She might be a smart cookie, but she was not a tough one. "No, I've never picked out a wedding gown. I know next to nothing about fabric, though I do have more than a passing acquaintance with the female form."

"I'll just bet."

"I think I know enough to help decide if the dressmaker has done a good job, if they'll meet the demands of the day, if they'll wear well."

"Like you've ever worn a wedding dress."

"And you have?" Not even the suggestion of scorn or mockery tinged his soft tone.

Shelley swallowed. She put her hand to her bun, then to her collar, then finally fidgeted with the tiny buttons of her blouse.

He leaned in, elbows on the table, waiting for her reply.

"Let's see..." She turned her attention to the paper in her hand. "Phone calls to the guests who haven't RSVPed for the anniversary party, to make sure their replies weren't lost in the mail. The decorations for the reception hall. Picking up the tickets from the travel agent, confirming that Mr. Taylor and Mrs. Winstead's sister will take care of the children during the honeymoon.''

"Shelley?"

"Me," she said, making a check and then another. "Me. Me. Me."

"You doing some kind of vocal warm-up before you burst into the refrain of the song you're going to sing at the weddings?"

She blinked, her face soft with innocence. "I'm not going to sing at the weddings."

"Why not?" He chuckled. "Looks like you intend to do everything else except conduct the ceremony."

She raised that legal pad she'd been clinging to all during lunch like a life raft. "I happen to have created a list of things for you to do, as well. That's why I was trying to arrange another meeting with you on the phone today, to give you your assignments."

"Assignments?" He said it loud enough to draw the attention of the other diners again. He flashed a smile, then lowered his head and his voice. "Lady, I haven't had anyone give me assignments since I earned my law degree."

She slid her hand under the top page and tugged free the next sheet, which she handed to him without further comment.

He met her gaze and held it.

She did not back down or so much as smile at him.

Finally he glanced at the paper. "Pretty basic stuff."

"You'd think so. However, given your cavalier attitude whenever we've spoken about this event, I felt I had to delineate each and every task. I expect you to take care of all this in Woodbridge."

She wanted him gone but bad. Why did that make him want all the more to stay? Was it just the challenge? Or was there something more at work here? "You are a handful, I'll tell you that."

"And I'll tell you that you'll have your hands full enough just taking care of this list, Mr. Perry."

"Is that so?"

"That's so."

"Well, let's just have a little look at this list you've come up with then." The paper crackled as he held it out to examine it. "Hmm. Done this."

"What?"

"Reserved the church. Did that as soon as we had a date for the party." He laid the page against the edge of the table and with one smooth movement tore away the first item on the list. "Rented the reception hall, too. VFW—it's the only place in town big enough to accommodate everyone."

"Well, those I expected, but…"

He tore the paper again, then wadded up both pieces and threw them in a long arc to the trash can by the door. They bounced off the curved lid and fell to the floor.

"Stop that. You can't just—"

"I'll pick those up on the way out the door," he promised.

"You'd better. I worked very hard on that list."

"Ah, yes, the list. Let's get back to that, shall we? Hmm. Done it. Done it. Done. Done." The quick ripping of paper underscored every word. "And can't do it until the night before the weddings."

"You're kidding. You've accomplished all that?"

He tucked the last strip of paper in his jacket pocket. "Looks like I'm through with my list. Now maybe you'll let me help you with yours."

"I told you before I don't need any—"

"Comfort and aid. I know." He let his gaze trail downward, then slowly up again. "Damn shame you feel that way, too."

"Why?"

"Because I'm going to give it to you whether you like it or not."

"Give it to me?" She wet her lips, touched her hair, blinked.

He sat back. He worked loose the knot of his tie, just enough to finish off his air of rumpled confidence. He watched her with a gaze so intense he could practically see its heat seeping slowly beneath her icy reserve.

She pulled her shoulders up, her rigid spine not

touching the back of the chair. She lifted her chin. "Mr. Perry, it seems quite obvious we are not suited to working together. Our styles are too different."

"Is this the same lady who was pretending to read me the riot act on the phone this morning for not participating more in this party planning? Listening to you then, you sure sounded a lot like a woman in need of—"

"My needs are met quite nicely, thank you. I require nothing more from you but a little cooperation."

She wondered if she had taken on too much, if she was worthy of the task before her. Could she do it? Or would she fail and lose everything? The words of the fairy tale she'd concocted the first time he'd ever seen her came back to him as he watched her now.

"In fact, the only thing I will *accept* from you right now, Mr. Perry, is the assurance that you will take my phone calls, do the work assigned you."

But what could the princess do? There was no one else to face down the dreaded beast but her.

"Oh, and be prepared for any last-minute things I might require your input on later in the week when I arrive in Indiana and—"

"Who did this to you, Shelley?" He spoke with quiet power yet she looked at him as though he'd just slapped her across the face.

"I...I don't know what you're talking about."

The fear in her eyes told him she knew exactly what he meant.

"Who let you down so badly that you feel you have to keep your defenses up all the time? That you have to go to battle over every stinking issue, no matter how small or how insignificant?"

"There are no small issues. Take care of the little things, and the big things—"

"Eat you alive like that dragon in the story you told the twins."

She pressed her lips together.

"You can believe me on that, Shelley. I've seen it happen."

"Why did you come to Chicago today, Mr. Perry?"

"I came because..." He remembered his determination to dazzle her. How he had wanted to impress this woman, with her killer wit, body to die for and her penchant for doling out murderous looks. And suddenly those reasons paled, seemed petty. He glanced down at his hands, then at hers, folded neat as a pin on the table, and he shrugged. "I thought you needed me. I still do."

"I need you to do what you said you were going to do. No less, no more."

But he wanted to do more for her. He wanted to say more. "You know, whoever he was, Shelley?"

"Who?"

"The guy who hurt you."

She dropped her gaze.

"Whoever he was, I want you to know I think he was a real bastard."

"Mr. Perry, this has nothing to do with you and me and the work we have to do before the weddings."

"Right."

"So, I have my list. And you have—" She glanced toward the waste can, then at the crumbled strips of paper littering the table "—yours."

"I do." He patted his jacket pocket with the one remaining chore in it.

"I think that just about takes care of everything until I get to Woodbridge." She nodded, then stood, collecting the check the waitress had left under the napkin holder as she did. "I'll call you when I get into town. In the meantime, I have a lot of work to attend to."

He did not stand. He thought that if he did, somehow, it might send the woman running off like a frightened rabbit. "I look forward to seeing you again soon."

"Thursday." She held out her hand as if asking for his word on the date.

He shook his head. "In your dreams."

"What?"

"I said I'll see you in your dreams." He tipped his head back and looked at her through half-shut eyes. "You do still remember how to dream, don't you, Miss Harriman?"

The blush that glowed from her neck to her delicate ears told him she did remember. It made him wonder just what kind of dreams she enjoyed in the unguarded solitude of sleep.

"I will see you Thursday," she rasped out. Then she turned and all but tripped over an empty chair sticking out from the table behind them. "I am so sorry."

It was the most heartfelt apology Wayne had ever heard a human being offer a piece of furniture. He couldn't help smiling about it as he watched her make her way to the cash register, drop a few bills on the counter, then rush to the door.

He had not done much of a job of dazzling her, he had to admit, but *she* had gotten to him on some level he did not yet understand. And he wasn't leaving Chicago, or Shelley, behind until he did.

Chapter Four

Shelley hesitated only a second outside the outrageously expensive bridal salon that her boss had selected to tailor the gowns for the big day. All things bridal set her teeth on edge with good reason. She would forever relate the standard "something old and something new" with "something borrowed"—her ex-fiancé's new lover—and "something blue," which was her when she caught them together.

However, today's reaction had gone deeper than that old hurt. It mixed with a new sense of...well, she didn't know what. Not knowing anything, especially something that had the potential to unnerve her, was not to her liking. Not one bit.

Shelley scratched at the hollow of her neck, then at the crook of her elbow.

She took in a breath of the scent of fresh June

rain on the sidewalks of Chicago and let it out again slowly. Everything would be fine. She'd pick up the gowns and get on with her work, smoothly, effortlessly, efficiently.

A small bell jangled as she marched into the salon, which she'd never been inside before.

The young woman standing alone in the parlor-like front room of the shop came around from the elegant glass case. She gave Shelley the kind of snobbish once-over perfected in exclusive places such as this.

Shelley spent her days working around people with more money than some small countries had. Snobbishness neither impressed nor intimidated her. Still, she knew she did not look, at first glance, like the kind of woman who frequented this shop.

She made a quick check in the huge gilded mirror that hung on one wall and reflected the image in the mirror directly across the room from it. Her simple white top was tucked neatly into her pants. No toilet paper on her shoe. She squinted at the reddish patch above her collar, then dismissed it as the result of her not-so-elegant itching fit before coming through the door. She cupped one hand over the loose bun at the back of her head, then swept a few wayward tendrils down to cover the spot she'd scratched.

"May I help you?" The woman sounded as if she doubted very much that she could.

"I'm here to pick up the wedding gowns for Rebecca Winstead and Danielle Taylor."

"The...? For whom?"

"Rebecca Winstead and Danielle Taylor. They may both be on the account of Mr. Clark Winstead—that's where the bill is being sent."

"I see." The woman glanced over her shoulder toward the champagne-colored curtain that Shelley assumed led to the fitting and viewing rooms.

Shelley looked at the curtain, too, but it gave her no answers. She rubbed her arm against her side in what she hoped was a discreet way of soothing a sudden itch on her wrist. "Is there some problem with the gowns?"

"No, I... Will you excuse me?" The woman took a step backward as she spoke, like she dared not turn her back on the likes of Shelley. "I need to get the manager."

"Fine. I'll wait." What else did she have to do, anyway? Only tackle her entire list of obligations single-handedly. "But please try to hurry. Any extended needless delay will throw me off schedule."

"I understand. Perhaps if your schedule is that tight, you should—"

"I don't need any help, thank you very much."

"I was going to suggest you come back later. I have a feeling this may take some time to sort out."

"Sort out?" Shelley asked, but the woman had already rushed behind the curtain that divided the front room from the rest of the shop. Great! This day had gotten off to a lousy start, and this did not promise much in the way of improvement.

She rubbed her burning eyes, wishing she'd had more sleep last night. Or, that when she had slept, it would have been more...restful. Her pulse did a little skip at the memory of the dreams that had plagued her through the night and the man who had inspired them.

Wayne had not followed her from the diner, nor had he called or come by her office after their meeting yesterday. He had not contacted her at home. Not that she'd waited by the phone for his call or anything. She always stayed home on Monday nights. And she had, on occasion, dialed the operator on other such nights to run a check on the line to make sure it was in order. That indicated prudent and sound thinking, she justified, even as she felt her cheeks warm.

She shut her eyes tightly as if that could hide her from her own embarrassment at her silly re-actions to a man who had no meaning in her life. A man she would only see once or twice again before he went back to a world she imagined very unlike her own.

Today she would be out and about running er-rands for the weddings, so even if he hadn't gone back to Woodbridge, he'd have no way of finding her. Just as she had directed, she would not see Wayne again until Thursday. Unless she had an-other one of *those* dreams.

"Well, well, well." Brass rings whisked over

the metal rod as the curtain was flung open in a dramatic *whoosh* of fabric and showmanship. Wayne Perry stood in the opening, a pirate's grin on his face and those blue eyes trained right on her. "It's about time you dragged your mighty fine—" he made quite a show of dipping his gaze to take in her backside "—you know out of the sack and got yourself down here."

"What are you doing here, Wayne? I mean, Mr.—"

"Wayne will do nicely, thanks." He held up one hand. "We're going to be working very closely together, after all."

"I'm afraid this is terribly awkward." A new woman, one with silver hair, rushed around the man in the formfitting black T-shirt, khakis and tennis shoes. "But Mr. Perry came to collect the gowns half an hour ago. He showed us his credentials as Mr. Taylor's law partner, so we presented the gowns to him. He approved of them, and my assistant is putting them in garment bags as we speak."

"It's all right, Helen." He gave the woman a wink and a cocky smile the likes of which instantly took years off the woman's mature appearance. "I was expecting Miss, that is, Shelley to show up so she could help me."

"Seems I've arrived a little late for that." Shelley folded her arms.

"Actually you're right on time." He walked toward her, one hand outstretched.

"But the manager said you'd already pulled rank on me with your partnership and best-friend status." She wanted to retreat a step, perhaps even bolt for the door, but his compelling gaze held her in place. "You've approved the gowns. There's nothing I can do about that now."

"The gowns, yes, but there's something you seem to have overlooked."

"I doubt that very much." She discreetly scratched a tingling spot under her crossed arms. "I've seen to every detail of the bride's wedding attire, from the proper slips to the perfect slippers. Every aspect head to toe."

"Hair to toe, maybe." He stood at her side now and touched her bun, then dropped his hand to the middle of her back. "But the ladies at the salon informed me that you forgot one of the most classic features of the whole ensemble—the bridal veil."

"I did not forget that. Veils are for vir..."

His eyes widened in promise of great fun at hearing her spin out her archaic little notion.

Thinking fast, she changed direction midword. "...irst, first marriages. It's only proper."

"Technically these *are* virst marriages, Shelley."

She glared at him and shifted her shoulders so that her back moved against his hand. That did not quell the itch between her shoulder blades, but it did make her so much more aware of his touching her. She tried to step away.

"And though no one ever confirmed it to me directly, I grew up in a small town with both these ladies." He moved with her, then went so far as to lean in and lower his voice, creating a mood of special intimacy. "I'd wager that on the day they married, they each deserved the honor of a veil." His gaze met hers, their faces so close she could see his cheek twitch with amusement. "If you know what I mean."

"Fine. Get veils. You approved the dresses. Why not go the distance and choose the head-pieces, too?" She started to turn to the door.

"Not so fast." He caught her by the arm. "Matt and Clark had a hand in picking out their wives' dresses, but I can't be expected to pick out the brides' veils all on my own. Not my forte, you understand."

"And you made it pretty clear yesterday you don't believe it can be mine, either."

"I did? When?"

"When you asked me if I'd ever worn a wedding gown."

"Ah." He nodded. "I was only trying to find out something about you then. Can I help it if you make me very…curious, Shelley?"

She fought to keep from shivering at the sexual growl in his words by doing the only thing that came to mind, commanding detached control. "I have."

"Have what?"

"Worn a wedding dress. There. Now you know

and you can put your…curiosity about me to bed.''
Stupid, stupid, stupid. You should have shut up af-
ter "Now you know." "That is…I don't mean to
imply—"

"It's okay, Shelley. I can see in your eyes what
it cost you to tell me about your wedding dress.
It's not the kind of thing I'd make a crack about.''

"It's not?" Could she really believe her ears?

"Let's go pick out a couple of veils.'' He jerked
his head toward the curtain.

The woman he had called Helen hurried ahead,
saying something about having narrowed it down
to three or four appropriate for each dress.

Shelley did not hear the exact details of the
woman's report. Her mind and her eyes stayed
firmly trained on Wayne as he took her to the next
room. Maybe, and that was a really big maybe,
she'd just met a man she could… *Trust* was too
big a word. *Share.* A man she could share a little
time with and not have to constantly worry that he
would end up hurting or humiliating her.

Helen, the shop manager, and Tiffany, her assistant, fluttered back and forth between doorways
and curtained rooms gathering the gowns and veils.
One would appear with a gob of net poofed up out
of a sparkling band or a hat with a flower and a
bow at the back. The other would shake her head.
They'd throw up their hands, bicker, then disap-
pear again as Wayne ushered Shelley through a

corridor to the place where he'd viewed the gowns earlier.

"I wonder if this is what it's like behind the scenes at a circus wedding?" he whispered to Shelley.

Shelley laughed. She tried to hide it, turning her face, covering her mouth, but she laughed, just a little bit.

Breaking through her stoic exterior even just that much warmed Wayne more than the googly-eyed gaze of any adoring female he'd ever had the pleasure to know. "I like it when you laugh, Shelley. Wish I could see you do it more often."

"I wasn't laughing." She scratched lightly at the side of her neck, then just under her collar. "Something was caught in my throat."

"Yeah, I know. A giggle."

"Let me assure you, Mr. Perry, I never giggle." She whipped her head around, her eyes blazing and her lips still parted.

Kiss her. If it had been another woman standing there, he might have followed through on the fierce raging instinct, but not with Shelley. He felt too protective of her. He thought too highly of her. He wanted too badly to take her in his arms and kiss her until her bun came unwound and her legs turned liquid beneath her. And he knew if he did that she'd reinforce her defenses tenfold so that he'd never get close enough to try it with her again. "That's a shame that you never giggle."

She blinked, but did not move away. "Why?"

He let his gaze fall to her full lips, then fix on her eyes again as he whispered gruffly, "Because I happen to think shared laughter is the most underrated of intimacies between a man and a woman."

Her lips formed an "oh" that she did not say. She laced her arms over her chest and drew her shoulders up. "I guess I've had an entirely different experience with love and laughter than you have."

The tinge of sadness in her eyes made him long to ask her to elaborate, but the set of her mouth and the upward tilt of her chin told him it would do no good.

"This way." He put his hand on her back to guide her and felt her muscles go taut as steel. "I asked them to leave the gowns hanging up so you could see how the veils look with them."

He led her into a large room lined with mirrors. A circular platform sat at its center. The thick carpet and white frilly stuff draped over every doorway gave the room the hushed feel of consecrated ground. The tacky furniture—fussy satiny stuff that included two thronelike chairs and a fainting couch—looked dragged from a place on the opposite end of the sacred scale, however.

He let Shelley settle into one of the thrones, noting how, even in her simple clothes with her hair all bunched up on her head, she seemed at ease there. Instead of sitting at her side, he took a place directly behind her chair. That way he could watch her face in the mirror and not miss one nuance of her reaction to anything said or done.

Why it mattered to him how Shelley looked, or what her response might be in any given situation, was something that had kept Wayne awake half the night. He'd made the trip to Chicago in a sincere effort to offer help and to work a little of his personal magic on the woman he found so intriguing. No big expectations. He just wanted some laughs and hoped to come away feeling that someone he saw as a truly decent human being thought the same of him.

But somewhere between the first glimpse of Shelley's glorious backside and the last look in her eyes as she'd told him to go back to Indiana, a subtle change had taken place. He'd gone from wanting to dazzle this woman to needing to help her break free of her past and insecurities. Why he had to take on that monumental task was beyond him right now, especially sitting in a bridal salon with Shelley, her posture rigid and her eyes wary but shining in anticipation.

"We've narrowed it down to two headpieces per dress, but Mr. Perry has chosen a third option, as well." Helen came swooping in, trailing ribbons and white frou-frou from each hand.

With the undiluted efficiency that she wielded like an ancient warrior handled his shield, Shelley pointed to first one headpiece, then the other. "That one and that one."

"That's it?" Wayne stepped forward. "You haven't even seen the one I picked out."

"These are the two I first recommended, Mr. Perry." Helen handed them to her assistant, who hurried off. She turned to Shelley. "You have excellent taste, my dear."

"Thank you." Shelley stood. "If you'll have the headpieces boxed, we'll just—"

"Not so fast."

Both women looked at him as if they'd completely forgotten he was in the room—a response he was not accustomed to getting from anyone and one that rankled him coming as it did from Shelley.

"My personal philosophy is that you can't make a good decision until you've sampled all the options," he said. "That's why I haven't gotten married myself...yet."

"You just keep telling yourself that's the reason." A sly smile played on Shelley's lips.

"You're not going to let me get away with anything, are you?" He laughed.

She didn't say a word.

"Okay, so at least pretend to consider my choice in veils before you dismiss it outright. That's all I ask." He took Shelley by the hand and gave her just enough of a twirl to position her to face the cascading layers of fluff studded with what Helen had called crystal beadwork, affixed to a delicate rhinestone crown.

Shelley gasped.

Wayne knew he'd chalked up a ten on the dazzle meter.

"It's so…"

He tried to appear modest.

"So…"

He tucked his hands into his pants pockets and hung his head, fighting to keep a huge smile of satisfaction at bay.

"So…" She walked up to the display, stared at it openmouthed for a moment, then turned to him. "Wrong."

"What?"

"It's so wrong!"

"Wrong?" Wayne looked at Shelley, then at the salon manager, then at Shelley again. "What the hell are you talking about?"

"Why don't I let you two talk this out in private?" The manager slipped out so fast that Wayne thought she must have had a past as a magician's assistant.

"There's really nothing to talk about. This type of veil simply won't do." Shelley gave a smug look at the spot where Helen had stood seconds ago, then blinked in surprise.

"Won't do?" Wayne folded his arms. "Won't *do* what?"

"It's too much, Wayne. Too frilly, too little-girl dress-up playing princess bride."

"And the problem with that is?"

"It's wrong." She thrust both hands out toward the thing. "Can't you see that?"

"No, I can't. What I see is…"

For one fleeting moment what he saw in his mind's eye was Shelley, walking down the aisle of his hometown church in a long white dress and that veil. His stomach lurched like a man jumping out of an airplane, not sure if he'd strapped on his parachute. He swallowed hard to chase away the sensation and waved his hand toward the shimmering creation. "What I see is fantasy. Isn't that what this is all about, after all?"

She cocked her head just so and honed in on him with a look that could have seared leather. A strand of hair flopped against her neck. "I happen to think marriage is about a lot more than that but—"

"Tippie."

"Well, it may be typical, Mr. Perry, but those are my beliefs, and I don't appreciate your making light of them."

"I didn't say typical, I said Tippie. Just then, the way you dug your heels in and glared at me, you reminded me of her."

"Oh, I—"

While she tried to figure that out, he moved in. "Try it on."

"Try… What?"

"You can't possibly make your mind up with it just hanging there like an old shower curtain."

"A minute ago it represented fantasy, and now it's a shower curtain?"

"Just tried to pick something you'd relate to."

He lifted the veil from its stand by the rim of the crown. "You seem like the kind of girl who showers pretty regularly."

"You flatterer, you. May I quote you should I ever decide to take out a personal ad? Single female, nongiggler, showers pretty regularly."

"Try on the veil." He held it up, hoping to entice her. He was right about this and he knew it. More to the point he wanted her to admit she knew it, too. "Once you've seen it on, you'll agree with me. It's exactly the right thing for the weddings."

"I don't think so."

He jiggled the headpiece to make the sheer fabric dance and the rhinestones and crystal beads flash. "You know you want to try it on. Every woman wants to wear one of these just once in her life."

"I'd tell you how condescending that remark is on so many levels, but somehow I don't think you'd get it unless I found a way to render the explanation with stick figures on your cave wall!" She ducked and spun with the grace of a champion boxer dodging a hard right jab. She was quick.

Wayne was quicker. He anticipated her move so that when she stood fully up, she straightened right into the frilly crown he had waiting above her head.

"There." He drew his hands away, careful not to tug or tear the veil, then stood back and met her eyes in the mirror before them.

He could only describe the look on her face then

as glowing with innocence, tenderness and vulnerability. It scared him spitless.

"Um, you know, you were right. This was a bad idea." He had to get that thing off her head immediately. "Obviously this thing is without a doubt, absolutely—"

"It's perfect," she whispered. She tilted her head to one side, just enough to make the fabric rustle.

"Perfect? No! No way. It's...it's all those things you said it was, um, too frilly and childish dress-up and...and something about a princess...." He looked in the mirror again. He tipped his head at the same angle as hers. "It is perfect, isn't it?"

She pinched one wispy layer between the thumb and forefinger of one hand and rubbed the knuckles of her other hand over a red blotch under her chin.

"Shelley?"

"It doesn't really go with either of the gowns, of course."

"No. I guess it doesn't."

She nodded, a depth of disappointment in her eyes that made him want to go out and slay dragons for her, to conquer worlds for her, to make her smile at him again.

"But it suits you very nicely."

"Does it?" Her cheeks colored. She wound a lock of hair around one finger.

"Sure." He lowered his head to murmur in her ear with just the right low teasing growl. "It has a crown, doesn't it?"

She stiffened.

That was not the reaction he had wanted. "It was just a joke, Shelley."

"*It* might be a joke, but *I* am not."

He opened his mouth to tell her to lighten up, but before he got it out, he remembered she'd heard that kind of nonsense from men like Baxter Davis all too often. "I never think of you as a joke, Shelley."

She blinked up at him. Her lips trembled and he could practically hear the words she wanted to say: *What do you think of me as?*

Not only did he not have an answer, he did not want to know the answer. They'd only come together in the first place because of the party they'd planned together. They had almost nothing in common. They were never going to see each other again after the weddings. They lived in different states, had different lifestyles and, he suspected, had vastly different opinions on the nature of relationships between men and women. If he doubted that, he had only to look at the hope brimming in her eyes as she stood there in a wedding veil gazing up at him.

To keep her from asking, or him from thinking any further about it, he had to act fast. "It also has one of these thingies."

"What?"

He raised his hands.

She started to step away.

He gritted his teeth. Differences or not, her inability to trust even the simplest gesture by a man cut straight to his heart.

"It's okay," he said softly as he reached over and pulled the top layer up and over to fall gently over her face. "I wanted to show you this."

"Oh." A childlike mix of awe and delight escaped her decidedly unchildlike lips.

"Just like a—what did you say? A princess bride?"

"Really? You think I look like a princess bride?"

"Yes." He inched forward, suddenly aware of how delicate she was, how he towered over her physically. He'd never noticed that before. Slowly he lifted the veil between them.

Her eyes grew wide, but for once she did not shrink from his nearness.

He'd noticed from their first phone conversations her inner strength, her sharp intellect, the wit she kept subdued by fear at letting anyone see the real woman beneath the polished image.

When he had met her, he couldn't help noticing the curves of her body, the rich color of her hair, her eyes, her smile, her soft skin. And now, as he pushed the veil back over the headpiece, he felt as if he was seeing all of that together for the first time.

"Shelley?"

"Yes, Wayne?"

He lowered his head until their lips almost

touched, then pulled back just enough to let his gaze sink into hers. "Do you realize..."

She raised her chin so that when she spoke, he felt her breath on his lips. "What?"

"That you have..."

"Yes?"

He stroked his thumb over her cheek, fit his hand against her neck and tipped her head in perfect kissing position with one smooth decisive gesture before he murmured, "You have broken out with one bad-awful case of the most unprincesslike prewedding hives?"

Her eyes popped open. She gasped.

Wayne fit his mouth over hers and kissed her more deeply than any man would ever kiss his bride standing before a church altar. Lost in that kiss and that moment, he never saw what was coming next.

Chapter Five

You have broken out with one bad-awful case of the most unprincesslike prewedding hives. If he hadn't chuckled under his breath as he said it. If his eyes had not glimmered with amusement as he moved close. If he had not pressed his smirking lips to hers, she would never have done it. But the combination proved too much.

In the split second she had to decide if she would give herself over to the heat and passion of this man's kiss or assert herself and show him she was not a woman to be toyed with, she reacted. Her hands came up. Her palms flattened against the solid wall of his chest. She pulled her mouth from his and shoved.

Had they not been standing on a platform, he would have staggered back a step, maybe two at best. Then he'd have found his footing and probably made quite a joke about her naive and futile effort. As it was, he stepped back, one foot went off the platform and down he went.

It didn't take a well-trained eye to know the man was in excellent shape. His muscles practically rippled beneath his black T-shirt, and even khakis could not disguise his cute compact backside and powerful thighs. Not that she had ogled the man...much. On him it was just so eye-catching that a woman would have to be dead not to notice. Her rapid pulse as she watched Wayne fall backward reminded her she was very much alive.

His actions showed the agility and quick reflexes of a born athlete. He did not flail about or lose his balance. He did not go sprawling on the floor, banging his head and tearing his clothing along the way, as she would have. He broke his fall with a well-timed lurch for the fainting couch and ended up sort of draped over it as if falling back there had been the plan all along.

She gasped and held her hand out. "Be careful."

"A little late, aren't you?" The state of disarray only made his hair more gorgeous. The flush of color in his face gave him a rumpled sexy quality that brought attention to the deep taunting blue of his eyes.

"Late?"

"With your 'be careful.' That's the kind of warning a Dominatrix of Decency like yourself needs to shout before a fellow tries to kiss you."

He let out a rolling laugh that resonated from the depths of his six-pack abs.

"I think you're horrible." She took a deep breath to keep her voice from wavering. "Dominatrix of Decency? What kind of talk is that?"

"Damned appropriate if you're asking the man who got knocked on his butt by a woman with a veil on her head and fire in her eyes."

"Fire in my..." She pulled the veil from her head and, with it, most of the pins holding her bun in place. "The only fire you've lit in me is under my tail."

"That's not without its advantages, I'm sure."

"I just want to get out of here and as far away from you as possible."

"Why? What did I do that was so bad?"

"You maneuvered me into trying this on so you could point out just how unlike a bride I am, for starters."

"I'd correct you and point out that I said un-princesslike, not bride, but I'm afraid of what you might do with that crown thingie."

"Tiara. It's a tiara. I should have known you didn't really think this was the best veil when you didn't even bother to learn what the headpiece is called." She fluffed the delicate tulle. The beadwork twinkled. The tiara gleamed. She sighed, then turned to put it back on its stand. "I can't believe you'd do something so rotten."

"Well, thanks for that much, at least."

"What?" She clutched the remnants of her bun in one hand and held it to the back of her head.

"For not believing I'd do something as rotten as setting you up, because that was never my intention."

"You certainly have a way with turning my words around. And I can see in your eyes that you think it's pretty darn funny, too."

"And you don't? Let's take stock of what we have here—a guy lying on a fainting couch defending his actions to a woman who just shoved him off a platform over one harmless kiss. If that's not funny, I don't know what is."

"There is no such thing as a harmless kiss." The second it slipped out of her mouth she wished she had never said it. He was going to have a heyday with that tight-lipped tidbit of self-revelation.

He looked at her intently.

Probably trying to figure a new twist on the dominatrix theme.

His gaze softened and the smile eased from his lips.

Maybe, she thought, he was going to do something worse than ridicule her. Maybe he was starting to pity her. She tightened her fingers on the smooth hair coiled under her fist.

"I should have known that, Shelley." Empathy, not pity, colored his words. He nodded. His chest rose and fell with a deep sigh. "There *is* no such thing as a harmless kiss. Not for you."

She dropped her hand to her side and let her hair

come tumbling down around her shoulders. *Not for you.* As if she was some peculiar throwback for whom even the most widely accepted norms of behavior were too brazen. What a silly, closed-off, inflexible creature he must think she was. Heat rose in her cheeks to think how right that notion would be, based on her actions ever since he'd shown up in Chicago yesterday.

The first man she'd met in years who did not treat her as a genderless paragon of efficiency, a big joke or an object of pity, and how did she treat him? "I am so sorry. My behavior was inexcusable."

He almost smiled, and that expression was even more compelling than if he had flashed her his heart-stopping grin. "Actually I thought it was kind of cute."

"You did?" Her pulse picked up. She started to scratch her arm but stopped herself just in time.

"Yes, and deserved. I was clearly out of line." He sat up and folded his hands between his open knees. "I just acted on impulse without taking into account that it wasn't your style."

"You must think I'm a drudge."

"I think you are lots of things, Shelley, but never a drudge. Like I told you before, I admire you a great deal. I don't often meet a woman of your caliber."

Why did that compliment make her feel like someone old and somber and untouchable? "I imagine you don't find many women like me."

"Don't get me wrong—I meet lots of terrific women. Lots and lots of bright, engaging, wonderful women."

He could have stopped two "lots" and an "engaging" ago. She got the picture. He knew a lot of women who were nothing like her.

"But you're a whole new class of woman for me."

"But you did say I reminded you of *someone*."

"Tippie." He grinned.

"So it seems I'm not the only one in that whole new class." She wanted to know she wasn't a total freak in his eyes. She liked the idea of him connecting her to someone he obviously had some respect and affection for. "Guess that makes me and Tippie in a class by ourselves? Or more like charm-school dropouts?"

He laughed. "Tippie is more of an obedience-school dropout, if you want to know the truth."

"And I remind you of her?"

"She's trustworthy, loyal, likes to bare her teeth and try to impress people with how tough she is, but underneath she's a sweetheart."

"Oh?"

"She's the best kind of friend a man could have."

"And you're saying that's what I am—the best kind of *friend* a man could have?" She should feel uplifted by his deferential words, but they only made her feel dowdier than ever before. She raised her chin. "So do you always kiss your friends like that?"

"Well, not the guys." He slashed his hand through the air as if showing where he drew the line.

"And Tippie?" She had no business asking that. However, she reasoned, he had compared her to the woman he called his best friend, so she had a right to know if she should expect the same treatment.

Wayne laughed. "Truth be told, I never get the chance with Tippie."

So this woman was something of a cold fish. No wonder he found a similarity in Shelley.

"Tippie always kisses me first."

"Oh?" Shelley blinked. Her fingertip went to her own lips. She swallowed hard, then smoothed her hand down over her throat, feeling that the hives had begun to subside. "I guess, then, that's one thing I don't have in common with your friend—you kissed me first."

"I know." He stood. "And I'm terribly sorry."

Terribly? Was that adjective absolutely necessary to describe his reaction to kissing her?

"We were just so close and you looked so...I guess I got carried away."

"Yes, well, the sight of a woman in a tiara and broken out in big blotchy hives will do that to some men."

"The hives. In all the excitement I'd forgotten about those." He bounded back onto the platform and peered at her throat and the open skin above her collar. "They seem better now. Are you okay?"

"I only get them when I'm…" There was no graceful way to end that sentence. She only got them when she was nervous? When she got too close to anything having to do with weddings? When she was sleep deprived after a night of hot dreams about a man she hardly knew? Each answer was worse than the one before. "I only get them when I'm stressed. It won't happen again, I'm sure."

"I guarantee it."

"You guarantee I won't get hives again?"

"That you won't get *kissed* again."

"Oh." Gee, why didn't he kick her while she was down, too?

"By me, that is. I promise I won't get out of line like that again."

She nodded. "Okay."

"Now." He clapped his hands together. "Why don't we see if the veils you liked are ready? We still have a lot to get done."

"For the record, I liked the veil you picked out very much." She took one last longing look at it over her shoulder and whispered, "Very much."

He stepped forward and placed one hand on her back, bending down to speak in her ear, softly. "For the record, that's all I wanted to hear when I showed it to you—to get your approval of something I've done at long last."

"My approval?"

"Since the first day when you realized we had to work together to pull this surprise wedding nonsense off, I can't think of one thing I've done to your satisfaction."

She could think of one. She pressed her lips together.

"Getting you to put the veil on, trying to make you admit it was a good choice, was a stupid idea. Seems like my ego just got the better of me."

"Not like *that* ever happened before, I'm sure." She smiled, her chin lowered as she wound her hair back into a bun again, struggling to make do with the remaining hairpins.

"You know, I see more of a resemblance between you and Tippie all the time." He reached up and pulled a bobby pin from somewhere near her temple and handed it to her, nailing her with his steady gaze. "You both get a little too much pleasure out of taking a nip at me whenever the opportunity arises."

"Hmm. I think I'm going to like this Tippie." She forced the pin in place and the bun stayed put. As she lowered her hand, Shelley couldn't help sneaking a quick scratch behind her ear. "You think we'll hit it off?"

"Trust me." He extended his hand to allow her to go ahead of him through the curtains. "Your first meeting will be like a walk in the park."

What the hell was he thinking, kissing Shelley? And while she was wearing a bridal veil no less?

Had he gone out of his ever-loving mind?

Wayne loaded the last of what Shelley had called party favors into the trunk of his car. The last errand of the day, and he couldn't stop rehashing the mistakes he made during their first hour together this morning.

Shelley wasn't the kind of girl a man grabbed or groped. Not the kind he could dazzle, then dump when things started to go stale. She was the kind of woman a man courted. The kind of woman worth taking the time to get to know, the kind a man fell in love with despite his every intention to steer clear of emotional entanglement. Shelley was the kind of woman you married.

Wayne slammed the trunk shut with enough force to make the whole car bounce. *Married?* Him? Not likely.

He rubbed the side of his thumb over the rich gleaming finish of his pampered Jaguar. He raised his head. In the plate-glass window of the shop where Shelley was settling the bill, he saw the reflection of a man who could rearrange everything in his life at a moment's notice. A man who could pursue whatever adventure suited his passions and pleasures without having to worry how it affected anyone but himself. He could not name a time when he had done those things, but he dared not kid himself—the potential was always in him. He was his father's son in far too many ways to pretend otherwise. He dared not let himself look at Shelley and wonder what could be between them.

Wayne had seen firsthand the pain and emptiness that consumes a woman who needs stability and substance married to a man who craves challenge and change. He knew what it leaves in its wake and knew how much it demands of those left behind. He would not set himself up for that, and he would do everything in his power to keep from bringing it on someone like Shelley—even in a short-term relationship.

"That's it." Shelley came out of the stationery shop with a satisfied smile on her lips and an uncustomary spring in her step. "That's the last item on the list of things to accomplish in the city."

He turned and slipped his sunglasses off to better watch her take the short walk from the door to the curb. The afternoon sunlight played on her hair while the breeze toyed with the strands that lay loose at her neck. With each footfall, her breasts moved against the fabric of her top in the same timeless, unmistakable rhythm that thrummed in his chest and points southward. Her hips swayed in the most innocent, unconsciously seductive way he'd ever seen.

"Everything else has to wait until we get to Indiana." She put one hand on the roof of his car. "So what shall we do now?"

"If there's nothing more we have to do here, maybe we should..." *Drive to your apartment, crawl between the sheets and stay there until some-*

one calls the police to break down the door be-
cause no one has seen or spoken to us in days.
Wayne cleared his throat, slid his sunglasses back
into place and popped open his car door. "Maybe
I should head on back to Indiana."

"Oh?"

"Tonight."

"Oh."

"I know we talked about having dinner together,
going over last-minute details, but it looks like everything is covered, wouldn't you say?"

"I have to admit, by working together we polished off my entire list in a day."

He tried not to smile too widely at her conces-
sion. He knew how hard it must have been for her
to make. "Then there's no reason for me to hang
around."

She cocked her head to one side and wound a
strand of hair around her finger. Just the tip of her
tongue slicked over the center of her lower lip.

Watching her, Wayne could think of a whole lot
of reasons to stick around. For her sake, as well as
his own, he knew that meant he had to act to put
some distance between them. "I can drop you by
your apartment building on my way out of town."

"No. No, thanks. I'd rather go back to the office.
I still work for a living."

He felt like a jerk sending her back to work with
his hasty decision. "I thought you took some time
off for this."

"With a corporation as big as Mr. Winstead's,

there's always something that needs my attention.'' She let her hand drop from her hair.

"I'll drive you over to the office, then."

"Don't bother. I can walk there from here."

He nodded, glad for the sunglasses that kept her from seeing his regret at their parting reflected in his eyes. "I guess next time I see you, we'll be getting ready to walk down the aisle."

She blinked. Her fingers curled over a pinkish splotch on her throat. "What?"

"You know, going over the last-minute stuff for the weddings."

"Oh, yes. Of course. I'll call you when I arrive in Woodbridge and we can make arrangements to do that."

"I may be in and out of the office Thursday." Coward, he berated himself for the clumsy excuse. Still, he'd rather be a coward with the option of calling her when he was good and ready rather than a brave man waiting around all day for her to reach him. "Why don't you tell me which bed-and-breakfast you're staying in, and I'll check there from time to time to see if you've arrived."

"I'm not staying in a bed-and-breakfast. I'm staying at Grant's Guest Lodge. I have a reservation for Thursday and Friday nights."

"Grant's Guest... You can't stay there."

"Why not?"

"Because that's where Clark and Becky are."

"You must be mistaken. Mrs. Winstead told me

specifically that she and Mr. Winstead could be reached at the Woodbridge Inn.''

''It hasn't been called the Woodbridge Inn for months. I'm not sure she even realized that or she just slipped and used the name it's gone by for the last twenty years. Either way, you can't stay there and risk tipping her off that something bigger than a plain old anniversary party is in the works.''

''What about the bed-and-breakfasts you mentioned?''

''Not much chance of you getting a room on such short notice.'' He clenched his jaw. Taking off his sunglasses, he looked down the street, which had come to life with the first stirrings of after-work traffic. Every ounce of good manners, common decency and masculine protectiveness demanded he rescue her from this dilemma.

She did not want rescuing. She'd told him so often enough. Even now he could see it in the way she stood, her shoulders back and her eyes narrowed as if she was running every possible solution through her mind. She would not welcome his help and he did not relish the possibilities that offering it would bring. It was too big a risk. It put too much on the line.

He looked over at her and their gazes met. And yet he knew he had no other choice. ''Looks like your only real option, then, is to stay with me.''

Chapter Six

Shelley squinted in the fading summer twilight to check the address on the paper once again. This couldn't be right. She stared at the polished brass numbers beside the heavy oak door, then at the name on the mailbox. *Wayne M. Perry.*

Standing back, she kept one arm clamped on her overnight case with its cracked handle and broken latch. When she'd accepted Wayne's won't-take-no-for-an-answer invitation to stay in his home, she had almost run out and bought herself a new piece of luggage. Who was she kidding? She'd almost run out and bought herself a whole new weekend wardrobe, right down to a frilly nightie-and-robe set. But practicality won out. This case had neat little compartments for every travel necessity, and it had survived three years of her clumsiness, even if it was a little worse for wear.

As for new lingerie? She thought of the large, comfy men's-style pajamas she'd brought, instead. Better safe than sorry, she'd thought at the time she packed them. But now, looking at this quaint cottage-style house, with its white picket fence and broad wraparound porch, she wondered if she hadn't misjudged Wayne Perry entirely. Maybe a man who lived like this would find sensible nightclothes more of a turn-on than lace and satin.

Never in her wildest dreams had she imagined that Wayne would live in such an old-fashioned, small-town-homey house. But then, she thought as she chewed at her lower lip and reached out to ring the doorbell, in her wildest dreams about this man, where he lived was never an issue.

The flutter in her stomach, which started with the memory of those dreams, increased as the bell rang to announce her arrival. Any second now she would find herself staring into Wayne's unnerving blue eyes again.

She clutched her overnight case to her chest like a kid waiting for the bus to a dreaded stay at summer camp. What was she doing here? Why hadn't she refused his offer to spend these two nights at his place?

Because this was her job, came her well-practiced answer. She'd committed herself to see this project through. She could not let something like personal inconvenience or anxiety over a potentially awkward situation get in the way. She was a professional and she would conduct herself like one, as would Wayne.

The footsteps in the house pounded as hard and fast as her thudding pulse. The sound stole her breath and her good intentions away. If she whipped around now and ran down the porch steps, she could be in the bushes under cover of dusk before he opened the door. She glanced back, hugging her pathetic piece of luggage to her.

She only had a split second to consider her choices. Like the princess in the story she loved to tell the Winstead twins, she could call on her strengths as the woman who always got the job done. Or, jeered the inner voice that often berated and judged her, she could give in to the weaknesses of the girl who had been bossed around and taken advantage of by men who supposedly put her best interests first.

The soft clatter of the doorknob turning told her the time to decide had come. She turned around just as the door swung open.

"There you are!"

"Right where I'm supposed to be," she announced as much for her own reassurance as for his.

"I'd started to worry about you." He stepped outside. "I called your office and they said you left hours ago."

"I had to go by the cleaners to get my dress for tomorrow." She decided not to tell him that she'd had three dresses cleaned and readied for the big event because she wasn't sure which one he'd like best.

"You're two hours late." He edged closer to her.

"I stopped for a little something to eat and to stretch my legs along the way." Four times. But he didn't need to know that, or that she had circled his block again and again getting up her nerve to actually go through with the plan.

"I was just about to hop in the car and go out looking for you." He curved his hand around her arm. There was a possessiveness to his grasp that fused reproach and relief.

She clasped her case more tightly to her body.

He readjusted his hold, and in doing so his fingers brushed the underside of her breast.

She shivered but did not pull away. In truth, she wondered if he wasn't the only thing keeping her upright. Her tingling legs and weak knees certainly could not be doing it.

"Well, you're here now. That's what matters."

"Why, Wayne, I think I sense genuine concern in your voice."

"You do."

Hope flickered within her.

He leaned close enough that even in the fading twilight she could see the amusement in his eyes. "If you pulled a no-show, I'd have to run this whole wedding wingding all by myself."

The flickering hope sputtered and died. She jerked her arm free, loosening her grip on her overnight case. She grabbed for it, but too late. It plummeted to the floor, struck the doorsill with one corner, cracked open and flung its contents across the threshold and into Wayne's entryway.

"Well, as you can see, I'm here now." She held her hands out as if to put the finishing flourish to her bag's big act. "You can relax and breathe easy."

"Relax and breathe easy it is, then." Wayne crouched beside her case and gave the spilled contents a once-over. "Nothing here to inspire a lot of tension and heavy breathing, anyway, huh?"

She snatched up her pajamas and threw them back in the case. "If you'll just show me where I can put my things?"

"Through there. First door on the right." He pointed down a dimly lit hallway.

"Thank you." She stood and started in the direction he'd indicated, her heels clicking sharply on the hardwood floor. "I really do appreciate your stopping me from ruining everything with that hotel mixup. I hope it's not too much trouble having me spend a couple of nights in your guest room."

"It's not—"

"Good."

"You didn't let me finish."

She paused outside the half-open door, an unwelcome feeling creeping over her. "Are you saying there is some trouble with my staying in your guest room?"

"No, I'm saying it's not my guest room." He stepped around her and stretched out his arm.

The heat from the closeness of his body warmed her chest and neck. "It's not?"

"No." He pressed his hand against the door and slowly pushed it open to reveal a massive antique cannonball bed that dominated a quaint but decidedly masculine space. "It's *my* room."

"Your room?"

"I think you'll be comfortable in here."

"Comfortable?" She stared at the bed—at *his* bed. Not only would she be staying under his roof, she'd be sleeping in the man's bed. She'd never slept in any man's bed. Why did her first time have to be in Wayne's? How would she ever get any rest in there wondering how many women had shared it with him, wondering how it would feel to be one of those women?

She struggled to drag in a deep breath, and when she did, it smelled of fresh linen, furniture polish and Wayne's aftershave. He'd certainly gone to a lot of trouble for a visit from a woman he swore he'd never so much as kiss again. Someone he looked on just as a friend and someone who stood to benefit plenty from his cocky idea of help.

She looked at the bed again and noticed a large robe draped at its foot. She gripped her luggage even more tightly. "I hate to inconvenience you, putting you out of your own room like this."

He laid his hand on her shoulder. "Oh, you're not putting me out."

She went stiff as a board and blinked at the sight of the huge bed. "I'm not?"

"No, it's my choice to let you stay here. I invited you. It's only right I should be the one to sack out in the study."

"Oh." She hoped he didn't pick up the unintended trace of disappointment in her voice. "Right, then. I guess I'll go in and get settled for the night. Thank you again for your hospitality."

"You're not turning in, are you? I picked up some fried chicken and a fruit-and-veggie tray at the grocery on the way home from work. I thought you might want a bite."

"A bite?" She dropped her gaze to his mouth and her hand went to the most sensitive spot on the side of her neck where she had imagined him nibbling in pure sensual delight. She swallowed hard. "I don't think so. No, no biting."

He cocked his head, his brows pressed down over his blazing blue eyes. He didn't make a joke at her expense, but he did not let her get away with the idiotic blunder.

"That is, no thank you."

"Okay. If you're sure."

"Yes. I know it's only nine-thirty, but I worked all day and then had that drive and tomorrow is a big day." She hardly took a breath between words. "So I'll just slip in here for the night and see you in the morning."

"If you change your mind—"

"I won't." She edged past him and into the room.

He opened his mouth and held his hand out.

"Don't worry about waking me," she cut him off. The longer she stood here the more foolish she felt for just standing here. "I never sleep past seven. I'll see you shortly after that. Thank you."

"Well, I—" He pointed into the room.

"Oh, don't worry, I have everything I need with me. You don't need to show me where anything is." She inched backward as she pushed the door shut. In the very last second as she stole a peek at his befuddled face, she managed a rushed "Good night."

Good night? Shelley turned to survey her accommodations. Wayne's room. Wayne's bed. A whirlwind began in the pit of her stomach. *Good night?* She doubted it very much.

What kind of Goody Two-shoes jerk gives up his nice, big, comfortable bed to a woman he'll never see again after tomorrow night? A woman who has already worked her way under his skin, but one he could never allow into his heart? A woman who would never, under any circumstances acceptable to both of them, agree to share that very bed with him?

What kind of man does that? The kind of man trying to doze off on a lumpy sleeper sofa in his cramped den with the streetlight shining through the window right into his eyes, that's what kind.

He punched a small round throw pillow. A cloud of dust rose from it and tickled his nose. He stared at the deep dent left by his fist in the thin padding, sighed, then tossed the cushion aside. He'd grown soft in his old age. Nothing else could explain it.

A few years ago neither the discomfort of the couch or Shelley's prickly disposition would have had any effect on him. He'd have gone after what he wanted from her—and gotten it with her enthusiastic blessing—or he'd have taken her rebuff in stride and sacked out on the couch content to think that it was her loss, not his.

Tonight, everything bothered him. The thoughts nudging at him of the woman fast asleep alone in his bed bedeviled him in as much of a real way as the metal frame prodding his muscles through the mediocre mattress. Why had she showed up so late and refused to spend a minute more with him than necessary? He knew she felt the same attraction between them as he did and wanted to fight every bit as hard against it. But why?

It didn't take anyone with more than a few credits of college psychology to understand her controlling behavior was just a defense—and a poor one at that. He saw through it immediately, and other women he'd known had told him he could be as thick as mud about that sensitivity junk. He thought of the story she had told the twins. Of the way she'd acted at the bridal salon, at her hint that she'd worn a wedding dress. He remembered too well the look on her face when he had confronted her and made it clear that he had nothing in common with the man who had hurt her so badly.

"What happened to you, Shelley?" He looked in the direction of the room where she lay sleeping. "What did that absolute loser do to you, and how can I help to restore your faith in yourself, in men and in finding love again?"

If she'd let him help, he mused. And if he wasn't so damn sure that anything he'd do that might draw them closer together would, in time, hurt her more than that bastard ever had.

It was no use. The mattress frame groaned as he pushed himself to his feet, scrubbing his bare chest with his fingers. He wasn't going to get much rest tonight. He might as well get up, grab a snack and check out the prospects on late-night TV.

He reached for his robe in the place he always tossed it, at the foot of his bed. Only a scratchy lightweight blanket filled his hand. His robe was just where he always tossed it—at the foot of *his* bed. He'd tried to wrangle his way past Shelley to grab it, but she'd shut the door so quickly he counted himself lucky to have escaped with all his fingers and any other protruding body parts intact.

So much for covering up for decency's sake. He stretched, hitched up his pajama bottoms and staggered out into the hallway.

The coast was clear. Shelley peered over the top of the open refrigerator door like a secret agent on a mission. Her gaze darted to the door opened to the unlit hallway beyond, then to the kitchen table a few feet away. To reach it without stumbling over, bumping into or spilling anything was her objective. It would take stealth, patience and a few moments to let her eyes adjust to the dark after the fridge door closed.

Grabbing up her glass of freshly poured milk in one hand and a small bunch of grapes in the other, she stuck a piece of cold fried chicken between her teeth. She hunched her shoulders, as if that would make her less visible. She felt like a sneak. A well-prepared, highly efficient sneak who could pull this kitchen caper off without disturbing her host or giving him the chance to disturb her, but a sneak nonetheless.

She thought of how uneasy and disquieted she'd felt lying in Wayne's bed. Of the troubled dreams she'd had of him touching and kissing her that drove her out of his room and to her late-night raid. She held the icy glass of milk to her cheek for a second. It did not cool her senses, just as this snack would not slake her real hunger. Taking a deep breath, she shut her eyes to blot all images of Wayne from her mind and let the fridge door fall shut.

"You know what we do with chicken thieves out here in the country?"

Shelley jumped at the deep rumble of Wayne's voice in the dark. Icy droplets splashed her face as the milk sloshed over the rim of the glass and soaked the sleeve of the terry-cloth robe she'd wrapped herself in before venturing out. She cursed. A very mild curse by almost anyone's standards, but she still appreciated the way the food in her teeth muffled the actual word.

Wayne chuckled.

She squinted, hoping that might help her eyes adjust faster. She could just barely make out Wayne's form moving toward her. Her heart rate rocketed. If she could see a darn thing, she'd look for a place to hide. She'd have to settle, she supposed, for simply looking cool and casual. Hoping to reach the table and set her plundered snack down before he switched on the light, she made one quick lurch forward.

Her foot came down on something soft and lumpy.

Squeeeak. A shrill cry of protest pierced the quiet darkness. Shelley's heart practically thumped out of her body as she leaped backward, sending the last of the milk slopping out onto her robe.

"Mummid!" She cursed again with the chicken leg still in her mouth, this time with a vehemence and volume she hadn't dared before.

A sudden click, and bright light flooded the room.

Shelley froze. Somehow she doubted she looked cool and casual with her hair in her eyes, a chicken leg in her mouth, and most of her milk on her bare feet and the cold linoleum floor.

"You know, Shelley, if you wanted to take a milk bath that badly, you could have just told me and not gone creeping around in the middle of the night.''

"Wreefing?" She glowered at him.

He shook his head.

She pulled the chicken from her mouth and tried again. "Creeping? You have a lot of nerve to accuse me of that when you had to have stood right there in the dark watching me raid your fridge."

"Me?" He tapped one finger into the center of his chest—his broad, well-muscled, *naked* chest.

"Yes, you." She forced her gaze upward to meet his mischievous gaze. "If you hadn't spied on me, how else would you have known I had this chicken?" She brandished the leg like a lawyer in some courtroom drama revealing the murder weapon.

Darned if he didn't project an air of near irresistibility when he looked sheepishly guilty and sweetly rumpled by sleep, to boot. He ran his hand through his hair and ducked his head slightly. "Maybe I could have made my presence known in a better way."

"No maybe about it." She started to the table again, remembered the shrill squeak and glanced down to find the offending object. She sidestepped the doggie chew toy in the shape of a T-bone steak and took a chair at Wayne's large round kitchen table. "And look what you made me do to my robe."

"Actually it's *my* robe."

"Oh." She ran her hands down the front until

they sank into a cold soggy spot and she winced. "Sorry about that. I guess it won't be much good to either one of us now, huh?"

"Too bad, I could have used it." He folded his arms over his chest and leaned one shoulder on the door frame. "Guess you'll have to settle for me as is. Hope the sight doesn't offend you."

"No." She made a show of shrugging as if the sight of a near naked man was so common to her it didn't even rate a comment. "Nothing I haven't seen before."

He cocked his head and his lips quirked to one side, but he made no comment on her claim.

She smiled a bit too sweetly, she knew. To compensate, she added a dispassionate once-over to prove her complete indifference to him.

That was when Shelley realized how low those pajama bottoms were slung on his hips. She blinked and blew a noiseless blast of air through her lips. Almost nothing held those relaxed, lightweight pants in place, she thought, skimming her gaze over the defined muscles of his abs, then lower. Well, "nothing" might be too drastic an assumption, she decided.

"Get enough?"

She jerked her gaze upward. *Enough?* How could she ever get enough of the sight of this man half-naked? He looked so domesticated and docile outwardly, but something barely beneath the surface of that facade sent out a wild predatory vibe. She wet her lips and swallowed down any trace of emotion before she spoke. "Did you say 'enough'?"

"Yeah, enough to eat?" He motioned to the grapes and chicken she still held in her hands. He pushed himself away from the door to saunter across the room and retrieve a couple of small plates from a cupboard.

"Oh, yes, thank you." She did not move her head but let her eyes follow him slowly until she felt sure his back was to her, then she stole a peek at him from behind. "Thank you *very* much. This will do me for a nice long time to come."

"You sure?" He turned.

She whipped her head around. "Uh-huh."

"Hope you don't mind if I join you, then."

"Make yourself at home." She rolled her eyes at her failure to sound even remotely clever and carefree.

"Thanks." He plunked a plate down in front of her. "I believe I will."

Seconds later he had a plastic container filled with chicken, the fruit-and-veggie tray and the nearly full milk jug out on the table. He refilled her glass, unfolded a napkin for her lap and rinsed the milk out of her robe—*his* robe—and tossed it in the dryer. Then he plunked himself, still shirtless and straight-out-of-bed sexy, at her side to become a part of her private midnight snack.

As with almost everything she'd tried to accomplish since she'd met this man, he had taken control of the situation right out of her hands. And done a better job with it than she had at every turn.

Funny, she thought as she munched on a plump juicy grape, she did not mind his taking charge for a change, even if it was over something this insignificant. She supposed she should analyze that reaction. Under the same circumstances a week ago, she would have searched herself for signs of the weaknesses she so dreaded—hoping too much for herself and believing too much in someone else. She had no desire to do that tonight.

Maybe the lateness of the hour had dampened her defenses. Maybe she had begun, ever so slightly, to trust the man with the laughing blue eyes sitting across the table from her. She managed a peek at him through half-lowered lashes. A delicious shiver drew her skin into goose bumps. She wet her lips, then popped another grape into her mouth. Or maybe she simply enjoyed the view too much to let her old panic and the propriety she used to hide it spoil this wonderful moment. It would pass all too soon, after all, and leave her with nothing more than one shining memory to sustain her for a very long lonely life ahead.

Chapter Seven

"I hate to say it, but this is very nice." Shelley pulled one foot up to the edge of her chair and hugged her knee close. She smiled shyly, dipping her gaze, then raising it to meet his again.

Wayne marveled at the obvious lack of practice her innocent flirtation revealed. It should have made him roar with laughter or at least chuckle and inspire a good-natured crack. Instead, he propped his chin on the heel of his hand and studied her face. "Why is that?"

"Oh, the good food, the charm of a homey kitchen." She acted suddenly fascinated with smoothing down the paper napkin beside her plate. "The company."

He leaned back in the chair, his arms folded. "Not why is this so nice. Why do you hate to say it?"

"I...uh..." The paper napkin tore softly under the pressure of her fingers. She looked up and directly into his eyes. "Is that a trick question or do you really want to know?"

"I really want to know." And he did. If he understood why she hated admitting she enjoyed relaxing, having casual conversation with him, he might understand her better. What he stood to gain from understanding her better, he was at a loss to explain. In two days she'd waltz out of his life forever. Still, he scrubbed the pad of his thumb over his bristled cheek and asked again, "Why is it so hard for you to savor the moment, Shelley? Why do you have to keep your sights on the plan, working for the goal and always keeping everything under control? Is it because of that guy? The one who hurt you so bad?"

"I never said—"

"You never had to. In my line of work you get to be a pretty good judge of character. You also learn that the harder someone tries to convince you of something about themselves, the more likely the truth is something entirely different."

"Kind of cynical, isn't it?"

He shrugged. "I'm not the one going around trying to make the world believe I don't need anyone's help or concern, putting up the sour-faced dominatrix defense to make sure no one ever gets close enough to really care."

Her back went stiff. She put her hand where her neat little bun should have been. When her fingers sank into soft waves, her eyes widened for a second. Then she tipped her chin up as if to say, *I meant to run my fingers through my hair like that.*

"*I'm* not the one expending far too much energy protecting myself from life and love. All the hurt and humiliation I assume has to come from participating fully in either." He'd hit the nail on the head. He could see it in the way her brows bunched together and the way she pulled her knee closer.

He was touched to see the dampness in her eyes and the tremble of her tempting lower lip. So touched that he dared not back off now and let her retreat again into the hard persona she fought so valiantly to project. "I'm able to look at things as they are, Shelley, hope for something better and laugh at the little things that often go awry. Are you?"

She hung her head.

"Then of the two of us, who do you think is the real cynic?"

Her head whipped up. "If I'm a cynic, it's not without cause."

"The guy."

If looks could kill they'd be hosting his funeral tomorrow in the town church, not a surprise double wedding. He did not back down. "Want to tell me about him?"

"No."

He scooted his chair forward until his knee brushed the edge of her seat. He could feel the anxiety beneath the surface of her frosty expression. He knew that expression well—the face of misery and denial. It remained etched in his heart from childhood. His mother had worn that mask for so long that after a while it ceased being a mask and became her reality. His sister, in later life, had succumbed to the same dilemma. Though he played rescuer for them at every turn for so many years, in the end he had been helpless to stop them from their self-destructive choices. But Shelley still had the opportunity to break free if she would accept his help.

That prospect had drawn him inexplicably to her from the beginning. That was what made him refuse to give up on dazzling her no matter how much she resisted. At least that was all he'd own up to tonight, sitting half-dressed in the intimacy of his kitchen. His gaze fell to the moisture on her lips from the piece of red ripe apple she'd just eaten. He pushed down the urge to brush that juice away with his fingers or to replace it with a long deep kiss.

Instead, he reached out and put his hand on hers. "I understand you don't want to, but *will* you tell me about him?"

She licked her lips.

Wayne shifted in his seat, forcing himself to stay honed in on her emotional needs and not his own physical ones.

She rolled a grape between her thumb and forefinger then set it aside and put her foot back on the floor. Bracing both elbows on the table, she exhaled. "His name was Ron Fuller and we were supposed to get married."

"Supposed to?"

"That's what everyone told me. Ron and I dated, he proposed, I was supposed to say yes and be thankful someone had asked me."

"That doesn't sound like the basis for an enduring marriage."

"Apparently it wasn't even the basis for an enduring engagement, but we got close."

He did not want to know but he had to know. "How close?"

"Everything was in place right down to the gown and guests."

"Close to getting married, not close to each other?"

"Close? To Ron? I thought that we shared, well, something—friendship, mutual interest. And my father and brothers told me it was the best thing for me to go ahead with the wedding."

Wayne shook his head in disbelief.

"So I went ahead, bought the rings, the flowers, even had two tickets to a honeymoon destination I loathed but Ron had chosen. The only thing missing was the groom—oh, and the girl he'd met at his bachelor party the night before." Her smile did not hide the pain in her eyes.

Wayne's jaw tightened. "That bastard."

"You can't blame him entirely—"

"The hell you can't." He slammed his open hand on the table. "If you can't blame the slime bucket for his own sleazy actions, who can you blame?''

She didn't have to say it. Her refusal to make eye contact, the way her shoulders slumped forward, the tremble in her hand as she toyed with a strand of hair like a scared little girl told the story.

"Oh, no. I will not sit here and watch you take that burden on yourself. It's not fair, Shelley, and it's not true."

"You couldn't possibly know that."

"I know more than you think I know." He stood and pushed his chair back so that the light over the table no longer shone on his face. His chest rose and fell with the strain of his effort not to make this about his own life's disappointments. "I had a mother who counted herself responsible for my dad's inability to remain faithful. I heard every plausible excuse imaginable for his behavior and a few that defied all logic and plausibility."

"Really?" It was only a whisper, but what depth of hurt and empathy it conveyed.

"Yes. And the worst excuse of all, the one that has you isolating your heart behind plans and precision and demands of yourself and others that no one can possibly meet, is…" He took a deep breath, then, with his face still in shadow, placed his hand under her chin so gently he barely felt it and tipped her face up. "The worst excuse of all you can make for a creep like that is thinking that you drove him to it."

"Maybe the worst excuse is the one I could have

made for myself. Why blame Ron for what happened? I had to accept the possibility that my own shortcomings caused him to look elsewhere for the things I couldn't provide."

"I can't imagine there is anything you couldn't give a man—from a piece of your mind to all of your heart and a hell of a wonderful time in the bargain."

"My brothers always said I had nothing any man would ever want."

"Brothers are not exempt from being jerks. They also don't realize how much their sisters might look up to them, how their teasing might be taken too much to heart and not shrugged off like another brother would." He winced and wondered how his own callow and careless words might have affected his sister. "I know I haven't always been supportive of my little sister, and how hard I've been on her over some lousy choices she'd made."

"It wasn't just my brothers." The single light in the ceiling shone on her rich dark hair as she shook her head. "My mom died when I was very little. My daddy really kept me sheltered."

No surprise there. "I'm sure he loved and treasured you very much."

"Yes, he did. That's why I have to believe he wasn't teasing me when he told me that men only wanted one thing from girls."

Wayne smiled. "Sounds like he used some old-fashioned scare tactics in hopes it would save you some heartache. I'd bet the world he never intended for you to take it *this* seriously.''

"He was a bit at a loss for raising a little girl on his own.''

"I thought as much.''

"But then, well, Ron didn't get what men want—'' she made slashing quote marks in the air with her fingers ''—from me. So he went where he could find it. How can I blame him for that?''

"Ron is a slug.''

"But—''

"Ron was a fool and a loser.''

"You don't even know him.''

He almost didn't say anything to that, but he could not leave her feeling this way about herself. Quietly, but with unquestionable conviction, he finally spoke. "He let you get away. That's all I have to know to make that call.''

"So you don't think my complete lack of sex appeal and experience drove him to another woman?''

He ran his hand down her arm to circle her wrist and raise her hand in his. "Oh, Shelley, if only you knew how very, very sexy you are.''

She pinched her pajama collar. "Nothing to create any tension and heavy breathing here.''

"Not from those pajamas, no. But from the lady inside those pajamas...'' He pulled her to her feet.

She stepped close, her eyes half-shut.

He could smell the soap on her skin where she must have scrubbed her face before climbing into bed. His bed. He slid his hand around to cup the base of her neck beneath the soft waves of her hair.

She put her small hands on his naked chest. Her fingers felt cool against his warm skin.

He angled his head, and when he spoke, his voice came out no more than a rough whisper. "Shelley, someday some man is going to come along who will love you and be faithful to you for all the rest of your life. You know that, don't you?"

"I'd like to believe it."

"Trust me, it will happen." That she had not moved away told him she knew what he wanted and she wanted it, too. He took some relief in knowing they'd reached this understanding. Someday her prince would come, but it would not be him. He'd made that clear, and she accepted it. "It *will* happen, but he won't be able to do that unless you're open to the possibility."

"I am, Wayne." She wet her lips. "That is, I want to try to be."

Some warning might have gone off in his head, telling him that even a kiss was too much to take from someone so vulnerable, but if it did, he disregarded it. He had wanted to kiss Shelley like this since that day in her office. Everything that had happened between now and then had only amplified his desire. In less than a second she filled his arms and he fit his mouth over hers.

Her kiss was everything he'd wanted and more than he could have hoped for, anxious at first, then passionate to the point of near abandon. If he had scooped her up in his arms and carried her back to his bed, then climbed in after her, she would not have turned him away. Her burning lips, seeking hands and the way her soft body molded to his promised him that.

And as much as he wanted to see that promise fulfilled, his ethical alarm went off. Yes, even years of practicing law and of prowling bachelorhood had not eradicated that one basic instinct, he thought, smiling to himself as he concluded the kiss and moved them apart. He had an obligation to protect those who could not or would not protect themselves. He drew the line between a roll in the hay with someone who knew the rules and a night of lay-it-all-on-the-line lovemaking with a woman like Shelley.

"This is getting a little too intense." He brushed one knuckle over her lower lip, still slightly swollen from the heat of his kiss. "Maybe we should just say good-night now. We have a big day tomorrow."

"Today."

"Yeah, it was a great kiss, honey, but I don't know that it qualifies as the kind of thing that makes today a big day."

"Today is the big day we've been planning for—it's almost dawn now."

"Well, danged if we didn't just spend the night together." He touched her cheek.

"I'd laugh if I wasn't so..." Her voice trailed

off. She cleared her throat, then gave one of the cutest phoniest yawns he'd ever seen. "Better try to sneak in a couple hours of sleep before things really get going."

"I couldn't agree more," he called out as she padded down the hallway to his room. He picked up an apple slice from her plate and took a bite. Standing alone in his kitchen staring into the darkness where she'd been, he swallowed the tart apple and murmured, "Things have gone about as far as we dare already."

Dear Shelley,

Thought it best to let you rest up for the party tonight, so I've gone out to take care of some last-minute things. Will be back shortly after noon. After a bite to eat, we can grab the wedding clothes and head to the church! Please make yourself at home until I get back.

Shelley lowered Wayne's note and looked around the kitchen. It seemed so much bigger with the late-morning sunlight streaming in and the table and countertops bare. She glanced around and saw not so much as a crumb of evidence of last night's snack. Could she have imagined the whole thing? Her fingers stroked lightly over her lower lip, and a quiver of excitement snagged her breath high in her chest. She couldn't have imagined that kiss, could she?

She pulled back the chair she'd sat in last night.

The sharp squeal of a dog's chew toy confirmed for her that it had all been very real. Kicking the toy aside, she looked around for any sign of the pet it must belong to, but her mind could not stay on that search for long. She had so many other things to deal with this morning, so many feelings stirred up last night, not to mention responsibilities for today.

She read Wayne's note again. "After a bite to eat, we can grab the wedding clothes and head to the church! Putting on wedding clothes and heading to a church with Wayne. If she shut her eyes and hushed the voice inside her head that warned her not to hope for too much where any man was concerned, she could almost imagine...

"Mrs. Wayne Perry," she murmured, her eyes shut. "Mrs. Shelley Perry. Wayne and Shelley Perry."

She pressed her lips together, the lips that Wayne had kissed so fervently last night. She held her breath. Someday a man would cherish her for all she had to offer. Wayne had promised her that. How she wished that she had awakened early enough this morning to look into his deep-blue eyes to see reflected there what she thought she'd seen last night. Wayne was that man. She just knew it, and tonight, after the wedding party had ended, they would come back here to his home, just the two of them and...

Bing-bong. Bing-bong.

Shelley leaped from her chair at the first chimes

of the melodic doorbell. For a moment she thought she'd best not answer. She didn't know anyone in this town, after all, but Mr. Winstead and his wife, Becky, and she was supposed to be hiding from her.

Bing-bong. Bing-bong. Bing-bong. Bing-bong.

The persistence of the caller made her think she'd better answer the door. Pulling Wayne's robe closed all the way up to her neck over her pajamas, she hurried to the front room in time to hear a big commotion on the front steps.

"I don't want to go to Uncle Wayne's house. I want to go to my house," a young girl practically wailed from the other side of the closed front door.

"We can't go to our house, silly." A boy's voice rose over the din of even younger children squalling at the top of their lungs.

Shelley hesitated, wishing Wayne was home to handle whatever mayhem had been unleashed on his doorstep.

"Why can't we go to our house?" the girl whined.

"Because, sweetheart—" a woman's gentle voice lent a soothing touch to the fray "—if we go to your house it would spoil the—"

Shelley knew that voice. She yanked open the door. "Marilyn?"

"Surprise!" Marilyn Taylor Smith marched inside. "Hi, Shelley. Hate to do this to you, but there's been a change of plans."

"A...a change of plans?" Shelley's stomach

knotted. Those were not words she readily embraced.

"Wayne around?" Marilyn swept into the living room, one of the Winstead twins in each arm.

When the toddlers saw her, they each reached out to her. "Aunt She-wie! Aunt She-wie!" they squealed.

Two older children that Shelley had never met but knew must be Matt and Dani Taylor's son and daughter trailed on either side, looking none too happy.

"Wayne should be back soon." Shelley stared at her boss's sister-in-law and the children she was supposed to be watching while the anniversary couples went on their week-long second honeymoons. "He didn't mention anything about your bringing the children by here, though. Was he expecting you?"

"Honestly, I wouldn't do this if I didn't have to." Marilyn handed Chelsea, then Celeste over to Shelley.

She numbly settled the two-year-olds one on each hip, while trying to make sense of Marilyn's rambling. "Wouldn't do what?"

"The kids. I know I said I'd watch them for the week. I didn't mind, really. I didn't even mind when Matt and Dani and Becky and Clark asked if I'd let them stay at our house this past week. The guys thought the closer we got to the weddings the greater the chance of a kid blabbing, you know?"

"*I* wouldn't blab," the older boy announced, sending his sister an accusatory glare.

"Marilyn, I'm not following you."

"It's just for tonight. You can go to Matt and Dani's house after the party and just watch them this one night. Dani's mom can take over tomorrow morning."

"Tonight?" She had plans for tonight and they did not involve children or staying anywhere but in Wayne's home.

"I'm sorry for such short notice, Shelley, but my youngest came down with a fever in the middle of the night, and she feels pretty rotten." Marilyn leaned in to kiss the girls on the tops of their heads. "There's no other way to handle it. I'm not even going to make the party, I'm afraid."

"Are you kidding?"

"Wayne!" Shelley's voice cracked. "I didn't hear you drive up."

"I'd love to stay and chat, Wayne, but I have to run. Shelley can get you up to speed on everything, can't you, Shelly?"

"Actually I'm not sure I know what—"

"Good." Marilyn patted the boy on the head, waved to his sister, who had hunkered down on the couch in a first-class pout, then turned to rush out the door. Just over the threshold, she jerked to a stop, turned and said, "Oh, there's just one more teensy little detail I need you to take care of for me, Shelley. It's nothing really, but, well, it's something that has to be done."

"Well, if something has to be done, Shelley is the one to do it." If Wayne hadn't sounded genuinely proud of her and if he had even an inkling of what she had already been saddled with, Shelley would have resented that remark.

As it was, she just smiled, though she imagined it was one of the limpest smiles she'd ever given anyone. Her one and only night with Wayne was already shot. How much worse could it get than that? "Sure, whatever else you need, I'm sure I can handle it."

Chapter Eight

Savvy, loyal, innocent, arousing, funny, and now Wayne could add good sport to the list of things he found so compelling about Shelley. He craned his neck just enough to see her standing on the side of the wedding party opposite him.

She raised her chin the way she always did when she wanted to appear fearless and above it all. However, the gesture lost some of its bravado when done by a woman in a lime - green, satin - and - chiffon, ruffled - within - an - inch - of - its - life bridesmaid's dress. Wayne smiled at her, despite knowing that she would never let her poised persona slip enough to smile back. He didn't care. Watching her step into Marilyn's place as a wedding attendant without so much as a grumble, he realized he still had a lot to learn about Shelley Harriman.

"Do you take this woman to be your lawfully wedded wife…"

Snippets of the minister's words to the couples renewing their vows faintly registered in Wayne's thoughts.

"…to have and to hold…"

He'd certainly enjoyed holding Shelley the few times he'd had the opportunity.

"…from this day forward…"

He wondered if he would ever really know Shelley or cease to find her fascinating, even if he took a lifetime.

"…keep thee only unto her…"

For a man who loved a challenge that was one of the nicest things he had ever thought about any woman.

"…until death do you part?"

And one of the scariest.

Wayne pushed his shoulders back and looked straight ahead. Promising to take care of someone forever might be okay for Matt and Dani, and Becky and Clark. And for Shelley. He had no doubt that a woman like Shelley not only needed that kind of commitment, she deserved it. She deserved the kind of man who could take those vows, all of them, and know he would never let her down on any of them. Heaviness settled in his chest. He was not that man.

"I do," both grooms said to the women they loved.

Wayne stole a glance at Shelley and caught her

looking at him. Her cheeks blanched, but she did not turn away. He lowered his gaze to the floor, then met her eyes again. Neither of them smiled this time.

In a matter of minutes the ceremony they had spent so much time and effort arranging and keeping secret was over. He should feel blessed relief. But something he could not quite name filled his chest and throbbed in his temples. He wasn't sure, but he thought it might be the first stirrings of how much he was going to miss Shelley.

"You may kiss your brides."

Shelley fixed her gaze on the delicate bouquet in her hands. It felt too "up close and personal" to stand a few feet away gawking as her boss gave his wife a passionate kiss. Besides, she could not look at the couples without seeing Wayne. And she could not see Wayne without thinking of the steamy kiss they'd shared last night, she in her nightclothes and he in almost no clothes at all.

Would they ever share another kiss like that— or something even more intimate? She dropped her head. Her hair, which she'd worn loose and wavy, fell along the sides of her face. She had worn her hair down to complement the bridesmaid's dress, she told herself, but even she was not good enough at pretense to buy that. She wore it this way because *he* liked it this way.

He had told her repeatedly how much he admired her good qualities. It wasn't the most romantic talk in the world, but then it might be the most romantic thing any man would say to her. Yes, Wayne's undeniable interest had boosted her confidence, but it hadn't driven her stark raving mad. She still had her bearings. Hair down or hopes up, she had to keep herself firmly rooted in reality.

The wedding couples had taken their turns heading up the aisle, and now Wayne stood with his arm extended for her to take. Gingerly she placed her hand through the crook of his elbow, then raised her eyes to meet his gaze. Whatever bearings she thought she still had melted like butter, just like her insides.

Walking down the church aisle on Wayne's arm. Short of wearing that perfect wedding veil and taking the vows, instead of witnessing them, Shelley could not think of a nicer way to wrap up their day together. Okay, she had thought of a nicer way, but now her responsibilities to the children made that impossible.

"Can you believe it's almost over?" Wayne's shoulder bumped hers as he moved closer to talk in her ear.

"Almost over?" What? The weddings? The time they had to spend together?

"Everything we spent all that time planning and arranging. A few more hours at the party and—" he snapped his fingers "—gone."

"But the memories will last." A leading remark to say the least. One she hoped would spur a conversation about other things formed over the past few days that they both hoped would last.

"You can say that again."

She put her other hand on his arm and started to nestle close to his side.

"I'll never forget the sight of you in that dress."

Only seconds before her shoulder would have brushed his, she pulled her back straight and fixed her gaze ahead. "Marilyn told me this dress is her gift to the two brides."

"Well, it's certainly more than enough dress for two women." They paused halfway up the aisle while the couple ahead of them stopped to speak to a guest. "You're really a good sport to put up with wearing it in her place."

"Good sport?" She supposed she should count herself lucky he didn't punch her in the arm when he said that. "That sounds like something one of my brothers would say to me."

"From what you've told me about your brothers, I think they'd say something stronger than that if they saw you in *that* getup."

"It's Marilyn's idea of a joke," Shelley explained in a whisper as she tried to appear congenial to the crowd of strangers in the church pews. "She made them wear dresses they hated in her wedding, so she thought the least she could do was find the ugliest bridesmaid's dress possible."

"She succeeded."

Shelley sighed. "I guess I can take some comfort in knowing I'll never see any of these people ever again.''

"Oh, I don't know about that.''

His smile warmed her heart. Her practical side warned against reading too much into his offhand remark, but her practical side hardly stood a chance when Wayne grinned and gave her hand a squeeze. "Well, maybe we can explain the dress fiasco to some of your friends at the party. That way if I do see them again, I won't feel like I made too goofy of a first impression.''

"Impossible.'' They started to walk again.

Her feet did not want to move. "It's impossible for me to meet your friends or to tell them about the dress?''

"It's impossible for you to make a bad impression.''

Suddenly she was walking on air. "So you'll introduce me around?''

"Absolutely.''

The first couple slipped out the open double doors at the back of the sanctuary, followed closely by the second bridal couple.

"I can't wait to meet your friends,'' she said as they reached the last pew before they, too, stepped into the church vestibule. "Especially Tippie.''

"Tippie?'' He frowned.

"Well, you said we were so much alike and that she was your best friend. I only thought it fitting that—''

"Shelley, I thought you knew.''

"Knew what?"

Wayne broke out in a laugh the same time they crossed the threshold, but still he managed to put his mouth near her ear and announce, "Tippie isn't at the wedding. She's my dog!"

"Miss Harriman?" Someone put a hand gently on Shelley's back.

She raised her head just enough to catch a flash of first one white gown and then the other.

"What's the matter, Shelley?" Becky Winstead's full skirt rustled as she crouched beside the lone chair in the women's lounge of the reception hall.

"Why are you crying?" Dani Taylor bent over to peer in Shelley's face.

"I'm not..." Shelley raised her head. Confronted with the evidence of her tears in the big mirror over the long low counter, she could not deny it. What a pathetic sight she made.

Her hair, instead of bouncing flirtatiously as she'd imagined, had begun to droop. Her makeup, which she'd applied with painstaking care so as not to clash with her outfit, was smeared with running mascara. And the dress...well, the dress was the fashion equivalent of the cockroach. This hideous creation could survive anything, including her personal meltdown.

Shelley Harriman, the poster girl for calm under pressure, for getting the job done when no one else could, for never letting anyone make a fool of her, had been reduced to a blubbering mass of helpless self-pity. And over what? A man?

A man she had dreamed of giving herself to completely in a long-overdue act of trust and hope, she reminded herself. She swallowed hard, sniffled and lifted her head. A man who had just compared her to a dog!

"What has you this upset?" Dani handed her a tissue from her tiny handbag.

Shelley wadded the tissue into a ball without even using it. "A dog!"

"A what?" Becky asked.

Shelley pivoted in the seat. "Wayne Perry told me I remind him of his dog."

"Tippie?" The two women in wedding gowns looked at each other, their faces drawn with confusion.

"And if that's not enough, he called me a good sport!"

"He didn't!" Dani crossed her arms.

"A dog *and* a good sport?" Becky narrowed her eyes, the short veil of her simple headpiece trembling as she gave her head a tight shake to show her disgust. "That big blond doofus! I have half a mind to give him a piece of my mind... I mean, well, you know what I mean."

"Of course we do." Dani spoke directly to Shelley's reflection in the garishly lit mirror. "No woman wants a man like Wayne to make those kinds of comparisons. Especially not at a wedding, when she wants his mind to be on...other things."

"Obviously he doesn't associate me with those 'other things.' Though he sure seemed to last night."

"Last night?" Becky cocked her head.

"In his kitchen." Shelley folded her arms, causing a top ruffle to flip up almost to her chin, then flutter back down again.

"In his *kitchen?*" Dani, who had been rummaging through her purse to pull out a tube of lipstick, froze with it halfway to her mouth.

"My goodness, Shelley, I had no idea you and Wayne were..." Becky cleared her throat. "And here we've saddled you with watching the kids tonight when you probably wanted to spend your time..."

"On kitchen duty?" Dani volunteered.

"On what?" Shelley looked up. It did not take a worldly woman to understand what the pair thought she and Wayne had been up to—and in his kitchen, no less! "Oh, my! Oh, no! No! It was just a kiss, that's all."

The two women in elegant bridal attire exchanged doubtful glances.

"It's just that last night he gave me a wonderful passionate kiss. Then he left before I woke up this morning, and with the plans and taking care of the children..."

"In case we didn't tell you already, we appreciate both of those things very much." Becky gave her shoulder a squeeze.

Dani, who had finally gone back to fixing her

lipstick, agreed. "Really we do. I wish my mom was available tonight to watch the kids. You're a saint to have done so much for us and now take four children on, too. Luckily they should be pretty worn-out. They were all burning up a lot of energy on the dance floor out there."

"I don't mind. Why should I? Apparently sometime between last night's kiss and this evening's event I went from being the kind of woman who inspires passion to being the loyal-companion type." Shelley started to fuss with her hair, then just let it fall where it wanted. "Woof."

"Don't say that." Dani set her lipstick on the counter. "There must be something you can do to make Wayne look at you in that light again."

"I don't think better lighting will help as long as she's in this dress." Becky gave the cascade of ruffles a shimmy with one hand. "Total darkness maybe."

"No, no good." Shelley picked up on the good humor with a sniffle and a smile. "With my luck this dress would probably just glow in the dark."

Becky took her by the shoulders and put her face level with Shelley's in the mirror. "Then fix it."

"What?"

"Shelley, you are the most resourceful, assertive, take-charge woman I know. I can't imagine you would let anything stand between you and what you want to accomplish."

"Maybe I'm just not sure what I want to accomplish." Her shoulders slumped forward, making the dress bunch in one place and sag in another. "Or what I even can accomplish."

"You?" Becky laughed. "You can accomplish anything if you put your mind to it. Clark always says that about you, you know."

"But he's talking about business. Business I know forward and backward and everything in between. This is..." What? Love? Romance? Sex? Shelley blinked and shook her head. "This is something I am uniquely unprepared to deal with."

"What's there to be prepared for? All you need is what every woman has. Brains, attitude—" Dani drew a small makeup bag out of her purse and held it up as if it contained the secret to Shelley's problems "—and a few feminine wiles."

"Oh, I don't think I could... Could I?"

"Yes." Dani nodded. "You pulled off a surprise double wedding while capturing the attention of our little town's most eligible bachelor. You can do this."

"I only know that if anyone compared me to that terror of a terrier—"

"Tippie?"

"She's adorable, but she runs Wayne's household with an iron paw." Becky laughed. "That's why he left her with a neighbor even after his trip, so he could get through the wedding plans without her making a chew toy out of any gifts—or houseguests."

"So she's feisty?" Shelley straightened her shoulders.

"Yep."

"And determined?"

"Doggedly." Becky grinned.

"And adorable?"

"Uh-huh. And Wayne is crazy about her."

Shelley bit her lip. She gave her reflection one more glance. This was a now-or-never moment if there ever was one. If she hoped to make Wayne see her as an assertive sexy woman, she only had this party, this night. "Ladies, do you think Marilyn would mind if I made a few alterations to this gown?"

"Mind?" Dani put her hand over her eyes as if she could bear it no more. "I think she'd thank you."

Shelley stood.

"What are you going to do?" Becky asked.

"I'm going to show Wayne Perry that I'm no dog, even a feisty adorable one. And that I may be a good sport when the occasion calls for it, but there's another side to me that has nothing to do with being good."

"Ooh, sounds like a great plan! But how—"

"Never mind how. Just see if you can get me some double-sided tape, a stapler and a pair of scissors. And let me borrow that makeup kit."

Chapter Nine

"Why can't you stay at our house tonight, Uncle Wayne?" Five-year-old Maggie Taylor tugged at his hand as he leaned against the back wall of the reception hall. With the music blaring and the lights dimmed for the dancers, the small girl looked sweetly out of place in her frilly pink dress. When a yawn that seemed to come from the very tips of her toes overtook her, she let go of his hand.

"Looks like you'll be fast asleep before your head hits the pillow tonight, honey. Even if I did come over, you'd never know I was there."

"I'd know." She rubbed one eye with a pudgy fist and yawned. "And I'm not tired. Why won't you come to our house?"

"Yeah, I think you should stay with us, too." Kyle Taylor, the child Wayne had played a pivotal role in helping Dani and Matt adopt, leaned against the wall, too. Even at the ripe old age of seven, his casual pose mirrored Wayne's to a T. "If you don't come to our house tonight, I'm going to be the only boy there. One boy and four girls. Yuck."

Wayne chuckled. "Someday you'll like those kinds of odds, pal."

"Not me." Kyle folded his arms, his cheeks red. "I'm going to be like you and never get married. Just have a dog and a truck and never have any girl telling me what to do."

"You'll change your mind about that, too."

"You didn't." The boy studied him in the unabashed way only a child can, without a hint of guile or disdain. "You don't need no girl bossing you around and making you feel bad if you don't do what she says."

"That's not the way it has to be, Kyle. Getting married involves a lot more than giving up personal freedom and always worrying if you're going to hurt the one you love." Had those words come out of his mouth? They had and he had meant them. Wayne glanced around the room filled with happy party guests all celebrating two truly wonderful relationships. He'd like to believe that celebration and those couples had motivated the subtle but real shift in his thinking about what marriages could be, but he knew better. He straightened. "You may be surprised. Given enough time and the right woman, even confirmed bachelors like you and me can see the positive side of marriage—even if we still doubt it's right for us.''

"I don't know about that." Kyle wiggled his foot. "Really I was thinking about that Miss Harriman.''

"Miss Harriman?'' Wayne tipped his head and squinted with one eye at the kid. "Were you thinking of marrying Miss Harriman?''

Maggie giggled and covered her mouth with both hands.

"No, silly. I was thinking about having her boss me around when she sits with us tonight and how I'm not gonna like it and how I wish there was going to be another boy in the house to be on my side.''

Wayne bent at the knees to put himself at eye level with the boy. "Kyle, did Miss Harriman do or say anything while she watched you kids today that upset you or hurt your feelings?''

"No.''

"I like her,'' Maggie chimed in. "She let us play wedding and I was the bride!''

Recalling Shelley in that sweet veil and the time the waitress had thought they were making their own wedding plans, Wayne couldn't help giving Maggie a conspiratorial wink. "Sometimes it's fun to play at that kind of thing, huh?''

"Kyle's just mad at her because she made him take turns. First we played wedding, then we played what he wanted.''

"Like I said, she's bossy.''

Wayne heaved a sigh of relief. He couldn't imagine Shelley doing anything to make the boy dislike her. He'd seen that in her the very first time they'd met. When he thought of her then and the picture she'd made earlier today with the twins in her arms, she had looked downright maternal. The model of loving kindness, a gentle, tenderhearted girl who would someday make a wonderful mom and—

Before he could finish the thought, a flash of green satin and long shapely legs caught his eye from his vantage point at kid level. In one instant his warm cozy maternal image of Shelley became something far more hot and intimate. He stood, slowly, his focus on the woman headed straight toward him.

If sex-personified could slip into a pair of pumps and go gliding across the dance floor in the VFW Hall in Woodbridge, Indiana, *this* is what it would look like. Nothing gaudy or obvious, but an enchanting mix of the sensual and the substantive, the innocent yet earthy. That was his idea of sexy, and Shelley had transformed herself into it dead on.

He watched her make her way toward him, knowing he was not alone in his admiration. Other men's heads turned. Women began to whisper to one another. Even the music swelled to the last crescendo before the driving rhythm began to fade into its finale.

Shelley moved with purpose and poise, as if she

saw nothing or no one but him. Less than an arm's
length away, she stopped and tilted her head. The
untamed waves of her hair fell against her exposed
neck. She crossed her arms beneath her breasts and
waited.

Wayne let out a long low whistle. "Wow."

"What happened to the pretty dress you had on,
Miss Harriman?" Maggie asked.

What happened was obvious to Wayne, and he
felt both flattered and frustrated by it. She'd done
this to get to him. He knew it. Payback time. For
avoiding her today, for teasing her about the dress.
Even, he suspected given the timing of her meta-
morphosis, for comparing her to his dog. And the
method she had chosen to make him suffer was as
delightful as it was dangerous.

Clearly she wanted him to want her in a way
that made up for every perceived slight he'd dealt
her today. She got her wish. He wanted her. But
then, he'd always wanted her, and after that kiss
last night, he knew she wanted him, too. But wanting didn't make things right or viable. Wanting
only made things...more complicated.

He wished she understood that. He had thought
she had when she talked about finding the right
man last night. He believed his staying away from
her today had sealed that understanding between
them. He indulged in an intent visual tour over
every inch of bared skin and satin-covered curve
of her. Obviously he was wrong.

"Well, don't you have something to say?" She batted her eyes.

The very unsophisticated nature of the gesture tugged at Wayne's heart, while everything else about her created its own tug somewhere lower. Shelley was playing with fire here, and she was not equipped to handle it. But how did he quell that fire without hurting or embarrassing her? He couldn't.

This woman could do anything and do it well, if she put her mind to it and got in a little practical experience. He had no doubt of that. She'd put her mind to seducing him, but in that area, she simply lacked any hands-on knowhow to accomplish the task without his cooperation. For her sake he simply could not cooperate. She was on his turf, and no amount of preplanning would give her the advantage here.

So he had to give her that advantage himself. He could not give Shelley the kind of life he knew she deserved, but he could do everything within his power to maintain her dignity. If that meant letting her despise and dump him, he could live with that.

"Well?" she prodded.

"I don't know about you, Kyle, but Miss Harriman can boss me around anytime she wants, especially if she does it looking like that."

"Boss you around?" Even her voice had taken on a new sultriness. "Mr. Perry, whatever are you suggesting?"

"Kyle and I have been having a heart-to-heart about his being the only boy in the house tonight. He doesn't like the idea of getting bossed around by a—" Wayne let his gaze dip to her lips, looking full and wet as if they'd just been kissed or she very much wanted them to be "—girl."

"Oh."

"He thinks I should come over and take care of them with you tonight, to help even the odds." He stepped close to her, so close he could see, even in the dimmed lighting, the delicate pink blush that rose from the exposed rise of her enticing breasts. "I'm beginning to think that might not be such a bad idea."

Her breathing grew shallow, but she did not back down. "If I can boss you around all evening, it might not be a bad idea at all."

"You can't boss Uncle Wayne around." Kyle's eyes grew wide as he spoke in a tone of disbelief, not defiance. "Can she, Uncle Wayne?"

"Don't worry, Kyle." Shelley touched her finger to the tip of the child's nose. "I have a feeling your uncle Wayne would be the first to tell you that my bark is worse than my bite."

"I knew you'd taken that whole Tippie comparison a little too seriously."

"How was I supposed to take it?"

"I meant it as a compliment."

"I took it as a..." She pressed her lips together, rather than tell him what she'd truly felt.

"You took it as a challenge." He fit himself

between Shelley and the two gawking children, then crooked his finger under her chin. "A challenge you rose to quite successfully, I might add."

"So, you like the...improvements I made to the dress?" she whispered.

"To hell with the dress." He slid his hand down over her bare shoulder, then around to her back and downward, stopping just above the plump roundness of her behind. "You could be standing here in that pair of baggy pajamas you had on last night, and I'd feel the same as I do seeing you in this dress...or seeing you in absolutely nothing at all."

Her lips parted, but she did not make a sound.

Yup. That got to her, he thought, trying to underplay in his own mind how much the words and the image they evoked had gotten to him, as well. He had to set his own urges aside and push on until she told him to back off and sent him packing on her own. "So are you going to let me come over and sit with the baby-sitter tonight?"

"Sit? That's not another bad dog joke, is it?"

"No." With one hand still on her back, he used his other hand to brush her hair back and lay her neck bare.

Her eyelids fluttered shut as she took a deep breath in a response that spoke of physical delight and expectation.

He reined in his own reaction, struggling to keep control of the situation. He had to remember that what he was doing was for Shelley's own good.

"If I were going to make a dog joke, I'd have said I wanted to sit and stay..."

"You're not staying the night, you know." She said that like a woman who needed convincing.

"Maybe even worked in something about rolling over."

"Over my dead body," she murmured, her head tipped as if offering her neck to his passionate kisses.

"Ah, so you're going to make me beg?" This wasn't going as he'd planned, but he was long past giving a damn about it.

"Beg all you want, but it won't do you any good. No matter how I feel about the matter, how much I want to..." She stopped and wet her lips, her eyes wary.

If they had been someplace even remotely private, he'd have kissed her until neither of them could remember their well-laid plans.

"I can't allow you to stay the night with me and the kids. You know that, especially not if there's any chance we might get carried away. In fact, it's probably best if you don't come by at all, just to keep things..."

He nodded. She'd turned him down. She had her dignity. He had his battered sense of nobility. And tonight they'd both go to bed alone, just as he'd planned. They'd both won. Too bad it felt so lousy.

Soft orchestral music poured out above the buzzing of conversation in the room.

"Okay, so we can't spend all night in each

other's arms. No reason we can't do that for a few minutes now.''

"Now?" Her eyes grew wide. "You mean... you mean..." She tipped her head in the direction of the parking lot.

"I mean—" he swept Shelley into his arms and onto the floor "—while we're dancing."

His arms felt so strong, so sure, so wonderful around her. As their bodies pressed close to move in rhythm to the slow sensual beat of the music, Shelley shut her eyes to drink in every nuance of the moment. She committed to memory the way his taut muscles moved with understated control, the hint of aftershave where his cheek met her temple, the warmth of his hand splayed over the small of her back. They swept across the floor with an ease Shelley had never felt before with any man. They stepped and swayed and breathed as one. For one indescribable moment she felt as though anything was possible between them.

"May I cut in?" The voice of Baxter Davis gave the edge of cutting reality to her fleeting dream.

Shelley opened her eyes to find Baxter grinning at her over Wayne's shoulder.

"Shelley?" Wayne put the decision in her hands, but he held her only slightly more tightly than he held his jaw as he focused on her and ignored the intruder's encroaching presence. "It's your call."

"I..." She hated to seem rude, to either man.

She did not want to leave Wayne's arms...ever. And that might well be the very reason she could use some distance from the man right now. Rising on tiptoe, she whispered in Wayne's ear, "Baxter is my boss's best friend and my superior at work. I can't embarrass him."

"I understand." Wayne nodded, moved back and slipped one of her hands into Baxter's, but before he bowed out of the picture entirely, he said something in a low almost threatening growl to the other man.

Shelley blinked at him.

Wayne raised the hand still in his to his lips, kissed it softly, then lifted his gaze to fix on her as if she was the only other person in the room. "Thank you for the dance. I'm going outside to get some fresh air now."

She watched him walk away even as Baxter yanked her close and took the lead in a rocking awkward dance movement that seemed designed for jiggling her body against his.

"You've finally let your hair down, Miss Harriman. I can only thank my lucky stars it was in a place where I could take advantage of it."

"The only thing you've taken advantage of, Mr. Davis, is my fear of making a scene." She pulled away from him as much as she could manage.

"If you wanted to avoid making a scene, then why'd you come out here looking like you do?"

Her breath caught in her chest, which, she realized too late thrust her breasts upward, accentuating her state of near undress all the more. "Am I...was it really that obvious a cry for attention? This dress and all?"

"Cry for attention? Miss Harriman, that outfit climbs on the rooftop and screams, 'Look at me! I'm not the dowdy secretary everyone thinks I am.'"

"It does?" It did. She need only glance down once to confirm it. Her cheeks flamed. What had begun as a daring reckless idea among a group of well-intentioned women in the lounge now felt like something silly and immature.

It was amazing that Wayne hadn't pointed out how foolish she looked. Or worse, thrown his tux jacket around her to cover her up for her own good, then marched her out of the room to save her from her ridiculous bumbling attempt at sexiness. He had let her stand on her own decision and supported that by taking her out on the dance floor. A rapid unaccustomed flutter started in the pit of her stomach. "I do look a little more camp than vamp, don't I?"

"You look the way I've always pictured you in my fantasies, my dear."

Shelley could not tell if the man was teasing her or trying to tempt her, not that she cared. Only one man's opinion and actions filled her thoughts and heart right now. "I look ridiculous. Wayne was too much of a gentleman to say so."

"Gentleman? Him?" Baxter scoffed as he whirled Shelley around, throwing her off balance

so that she had to cling to him to remain upright.
"You wouldn't think he was such a gentleman if
you heard what he said to me before he stormed
out of here."

"What?" Shelley clutched at her partner's
shoulders and stumbled to a standstill. "What did
he say to you?"

"He said I could have this dance, but not to get
any ideas. You were going home with him."

"What?"

"He said you were going home with him.
Frankly, Miss Harriman, I think you could do better."

"I never said I'd... He had no right to say that."

"If you'll pardon my saying so, he doesn't strike
me as the kind overly concerned with rights when
he sees something he wants. Remember how he
acted that day in your office?"

She did remember. She remembered every time
he charged in and started doing things his way,
making her decisions for her. From that first night
to the restaurant, the dresses and veils, and the
"invitation" to stay at his home last night, he had
imposed his choices on her, paying respect to her
ability to manage things herself in words but not
in actions, where it counted.

The lights dipped and swirled around Shelley,
but her feet did not move. She clenched her teeth.
She let her breath out slowly. Then she raised her
chin and slipped back into the studied persona that
suited her far more than satin and seduction.

"There are two things I cannot abide from a man, Baxter."

"Only two?"

She ignored his leering. "One is to have him think he can tell me what to do with my life. The second is to play me for a fool. Tonight it's time I realized that Wayne Perry has done both ever since we began working on this project together."

"What are you going to do about that?"

"Do? Nothing. What can I do?" She glanced around the room and spotted the place where Wayne had stood with Kyle and Maggie. The two children sat slumped in chairs, looking tired and bored. "I can't change what happened between Wayne and me. I can only fulfill my obligations here tonight and then go on with my life back in Chicago."

"What about this Wayne fellow? Don't you want to give him hell like you always do me when I cross the line?"

"What I want to give Wayne..." Their kiss, the dance, the hope she'd had of sharing his bed with him, all flitted through her mind. "What I want to give Wayne is irrelevant. What I won't give him is the satisfaction of a dramatic goodbye."

What the hell had he been thinking? One minute he wanted to use the threat of real intimacy to cause Shelley to back down of her own accord. A few turns on the dance floor with the lady in his arms cut short by the arrival of that Davis jerk, and he was ready to undo his night's one good deed.

He shoved his hands into the pockets of his tux, looked up at the immense field of stars twinkling in the night sky and swore under his breath. If he had any sense at all, he'd head home right now and forget he ever met— "Shelley?"

The lime shoes and the way her hair straggled down from a haphazard bun gave away the figure creeping out of the hall with a frayed pink baby blanket dangling over her shoulder.

"Shelley, is that you?" Gravel from the parking lot crunched under her feet as he hurried toward the retreating woman. "Why did you put your hair back up? Where are you going?"

"Shh." She turned just enough for him to see the sleeping two-year-old she held.

"Sorry." Wayne froze where he stood.

Instead of marching on to the car where he and Marilyn had transferred the car seats earlier today, Shelley hesitated. A wisp of angelic baby hair clung to her cheek. One hand cradled the child's head to her shoulder, the other supported the baby's bottom and still managed to hang on to a diaper bag.

She looked so natural that way, so perfect, that it made his gut ache just to witness it and know he would never be a part of seeing her like that again.

"I'm taking the kids home now. They're worn-out."

"Would you like me to—"

"No."

"Shelley, you're not mad about...everything, are you?"

"No."

He could take some comfort in that, he supposed.

"Not about *everything*."

He couldn't help himself. He smiled at that. She wouldn't have made that important addition as recently as a week ago. She wasn't willing to play the dutiful drudge anymore. For that much he could congratulate himself. He *had* helped her even if he knew he could not rescue her completely.

"For the record, I'm less angry than I am just coming to my senses."

He nodded. That was what he'd wanted all along, wasn't it? Still, he felt like a total heel. "If it helps, I'm really sorry things couldn't work out differently."

"I have to get the kids to the Taylors' house now."

"I'd be glad to—"

"No." She spoke loudly enough to rouse the child slightly. With sweet soothing words she quieted the little one.

She did it so well. She did everything so well. That ache in his gut twisted, and his throat felt as if someone had grabbed it and begun to squeeze and squeeze. "Shelley, it wouldn't be so bad, would it, if you let me help you with the kids? It's just for one night, after all.''

Behind him, the hushed bustle of the other kids giving goodbye kisses eased into the edge of his consciousness. Dani and Matt, and Becky and Clark promised to call, gave last-minute instructions. Wayne did not take his eyes from Shelley's.

The families trundled past and began tucking kids into car seats and fastening safety belts in Shelley's car.

He took a step toward her, his hand outstretched. ''Shelley, I—''

''No, Wayne. I meant it.'' She started to move away, then suddenly turned, her face sad but serene. ''The last thing on earth I want or need, Wayne, is any help from you.''

Chapter Ten

Not even time for the eleven o'clock news, and Shelley already had tucked the kids in, twice, and read them stories, twice. She'd glanced out the front window half a dozen times to see if some sound was a car pulling into the Taylors' driveway. Finally she'd pulled on her dull roomy jammies and settled on the couch for the night. What else was she going to do? Sleep did not seem a likely option.

She tossed the TV changer onto the coffee table and curled her bare feet beneath her on the big comfy couch. Photographs looked down on her from the walls of the family room, captured memories of life's sweetest moments. Toys spilled from the brightly painted chest in the corner. Two pairs of shoes, one a woman's, one a man's, lay jumbled by the empty fireplace.

It felt odd to be in a strange home caring for someone else's children, and yet it appealed to her. Here, where she had no history, no collection of disappointments and certainly no memories of a certain warm conversation and hot kiss, she could let her dreams run free. She shut her eyes and tried to imagine this as her home and family, but she couldn't pull it off. Heart heavy, she sighed. How could she have those things without first finding love and a relationship based on passion, shared goals and mutual respect? Those things she had hoped she might find and cultivate with...

She hugged her knees close and bit her lip, her eyes on the door. The party was probably still going strong, probably still alive with food and drink, laughter and dancing. Wayne would have found no shortage of partners to share all those things and much more tonight. She knew that much.

She looked at the clock on the mantel. The hall would stay bustling for another hour at least, maybe two. The anniversary couples would have left shortly after she did, but the hall was theirs until after midnight. Dani Taylor's mom had promised to stay until the last person went home, which was one reason she could not baby-sit the children. That and the fact that she had to clean up the church first thing in the morning so they could have another wedding there Saturday afternoon. This was the wedding season, they'd told Shelley when she'd made the arrangements for the surprise festivities. *Wedding season.*

She coiled a tendril of hair around her finger, unable to keep from thinking of the thrill about making wedding plans, even though they weren't her own. And the magical but bittersweet feeling of seeing herself in the perfect wedding veil with Wayne at her side.

Wayne. What had gone wrong there? Why hadn't it worked out? If not the happily-ever-after kind of working out, why couldn't they at least have made a deeper connection?

How often during the time they worked together had she hoped she might at last be ready to trust again, to step back into life and embrace the chance of love? Now she wondered if she had been so nearly ready at all. She hugged her knees still closer, bowed her head and squeezed her eyes until the tears began to flow. What was so awfully wrong with her that she had failed both herself and Wayne on those counts?

If only he had talked to her more. If only he had stopped trying to play knight in shining armor come to rescue her from even the simplest dilemmas. If only he had been able to share his feelings and help her to understand why he seemed to want her one moment, then reject her the next. If only he was here now.

The sharp *chirrrp* of the phone made her heart practically leap from her chest. Could it be? She clutched her pajama top closed at the neck and clambered up off the couch.

The phone rang again.

From upstairs she heard a child cough.

She hesitated.

All went quiet again overhead.

The phone chirped again, sounding somehow more insistent than before.

She reached for it, her eyes shut and a wordless prayer on her lips that if it was who she hoped it was she would handle things with dignity and grace. "This is the Taylor residence."

"Shelley? It's Marilyn. I didn't wake you, did I?"

"Um, no." Not from anything but a pointless daydream, she thought. "No, I was still up."

"Good. I called the VFW Hall first. They said you'd taken the kids home and that Dani and Matt and Becky and Clark had gone, too."

"They had to get to Indianapolis to catch the flights for the second honeymoons. The Winsteads' plane should have taken off already and the Taylors' will have boarded, at the very least. So if you needed to get in touch with them, it might be some time before we could arrange—"

"Gee, I hope that's not necessary. I really hate the idea of calling them home unless we're absolutely sure."

"Calling them *home?* Unless we're sure?" Shelley gripped the phone. "Sure about what?"

"Oh!" Marilyn's laugh gave no sign of real amusement. "I guess I haven't told you yet, have I?"

"Told me what?"

"I feel awful about this. After I made you wear that dress and— How did that work out, by the way? Were the girls really surprised?"

"Told me what, Marilyn?"

"Best to err on the side of caution, I always say. And doubly so when children are involved."

Shelley twisted the phone chord around her fingers, her leg jiggling with reined-in nervous energy. She could hardly use her tough-as-nails business routine to wring whatever her boss's sister-in-law was trying to say out of her.

Another cough from upstairs followed by a bit of fussing from the twins' room.

"Marilyn, if you don't mind, I need—"

"The kids have been exposed to chicken pox."

She could have gasped or groaned or banged her head against the wall—or better yet banged the phone receiver against the wall so Marilyn could better share in the frustration. But she didn't. She wouldn't. That wasn't her. Drawing in a deep breath, she threw herself into facing and fixing the problem with levelheaded efficiency.

"Details, Marilyn, I need details."

"Well, I do know that Kyle and Maggie have had them—my oldest gave it to them three summers ago before my youngest was born. So you don't have to worry about them coming down with it, if that's what it is."

"What do you mean?"

"So far, no spots. Could be they've got bad colds or flu of some kind. Say, are you there alone with the kids? Because if you are you probably better get help over there pronto."

"I am quite capable of caring for—"

"Have you had the chicken pox?"

"Um, I think…no, I can't say for sure. I remember getting red spots when I was a kid, but it could have been measles or just a rash."

"If you haven't been exposed to it, *don't*. Adult-onset chicken pox can be very serious."

"Maybe it's not chicken pox."

"And four kids with the flu would be easier for one person to handle how? You need to get someone in there to help."

"Someone in to help?" Shelley didn't know anyone in town but Wayne.

She had heard the warning "Be careful what you wish for, you might get it" many times in her life. Until this moment she'd never fully appreciated the sentiment behind it. A few minutes ago she'd wished Wayne was with her. Now she had to place a phone call and make that wish come true.

From the very beginning of their working together, Wayne had tried to show that he knew what was best and she had fought to maintain her independence. She had rebuffed his take-charge attitude at every turn, right down to the final words she'd said to him tonight. *The last thing on earth I want or need, Wayne, is help from you.*

As she hung up the phone, her shoulders slumped forward. She glanced toward the stairs

where the kids lay sleeping. She listened for another cough or some sign she should rush up there.
Silence greeted her. How long could that last? If
one twin roused with the discomfort of a fever or
worse, the other would soon follow. Then there
were Kyle and Maggie. They'd probably rather
have the familiar face of the man they called uncle
close at hand if they should wake up sick and mis-
erable.

She stared at the phone, bit her lip, scratched her
neck, then sighed. She had no choice. She had to
make the call and ask for Wayne's help, because
despite her bold proclamation, she needed a knight
in shining armor and she needed him now.

Wayne rang the bell and when he didn't get an
instantaneous response, pounded on the door.

From somewhere around his ankles Tippie
barked.

Shelley had finally asked him for help. It had
taken six weeks, four kids, two cases of potential
chicken pox and one moment of desperation, but
she had finally done it. She'd proved the point he'd
made to the young man in the coffee shop in Chicago: *Deep down, when it's all said and done,
women still want a man of action.*

Despite her protests, when it got right down to
it, Shelley wanted him to take the helm. The un-
certain little princess in her needed him to do that,
now more than ever. He no longer had any doubt
of it. "Shelley?" He thudded the side of his fist

against the door again. "Shelley, it's me. Open up. I'm here to—"

His fist met air as the door swung inward to reveal Shelley in bare feet, jeans and her pajama top. "Would you pipe down? Don't you know how late it is?"

"Sorry, I—"

Tippie snapped off a quick bark and marched into the house as if she owned the place.

Shelley questioned the action with nothing more than a tilt of her head.

Tippie turned in a perfect circle on the entryway tile, plunked down and cocked her own head in a perfect mirror of Shelley's pose.

"Tippie, I presume?"

Wayne tucked his hands in his pockets. "I left the party right after the guests of honor did."

"Oh?" Her eyes flashed with something he could only call relief, then went cool.

He wished he had the right to enjoy her reaction. But he'd given up that privilege for her own good, and now, with necessity making them roomies for another night, he had to maintain his resolve to remain detached more than ever. "Yes. Postparty letdown, I guess. All that planning and work and then—" he snapped his fingers "—over."

She nodded.

"So I went home, but the house seemed, I don't know, empty somehow."

"You mean without my shining presence?" The

joking in her tone did not mask the questioning truth in her words.

Wayne shuffled his feet on the doorstep. "So I went to my neighbors, who were watching Tippie, and brought her home."

"Oh." Shelley looked down at the spunky little terrier with her expectant gaze fixed on Wayne. "So it works both ways."

"What?"

She smiled, but sadness lingered in her eyes. "I reminded you of Tippie, so you thought Tippie could just as easily take my place at keeping you company."

Not by a long shot. He thought it but didn't say it. He didn't say anything.

Neither did Shelley.

The night air prickled on the back of Wayne's neck.

Shelley started one after another of her usual nervous gestures, caught herself and finally folded her arms under her breasts.

Backlit by the warm glow of the homey interior, with moonlight on her face and casting soft highlights in her enticingly disheveled hair, she looked every bit the fragile soul he'd first pegged her to be. He knew he had done the right thing in trying to build her up; she had grown because of his tough and sometimes tender influence. He also knew she could not have grown enough for him to risk anything more than friendship with her.

"You going to ask me in, or do you want me

to get a ladder and watch the kids from outside the bedroom windows?"

"Oh, yes. Sure. Come in." She stepped aside and made a sweep with her arm. "Come in."

As soon as he was fully inside, Tippie hopped up and began trotting from room to room. Obviously desperate to make small talk, Shelley watched intently, then asked, "Why is she doing that?"

"I don't know. Maybe she's preplanning where she's going to wet the carpet."

"Funny." If she had been any more like Tippie, she'd have growled at him.

He laughed. "Look, she probably didn't want to check the place out until you let me in. She just felt more secure knowing I was here if she needed me."

"Subtlety is not your forte, is it?" She put her hands on her hips. "Don't think I don't get the whole puppy-parallel-meaning thing you're trying to pull. Two can play at that. I say Tippie is taking things into her own hands."

"Shouldn't that be paws?"

"She's in a new situation, but that does not mean she's giving up control. In fact, new situations are when she knows she has to take charge and not rely on anyone else."

"Could be. She might be a little happier, though, if she'd relax and trust that I'm always going to make sure she's safe and cared for."

"Maybe she wants to make sure of those things

herself.'' Shelley rubbed her knuckles under her chin.

''Like that princess in the story you told the twins?''

''Exactly. That princess could stand up to the dragon on her own because she was strong enough and smart enough to do it. That's how... Tippie is.''

''I don't know if I'd call standing up to a dragon by yourself smart.'' He gave her a conciliatory grin. ''Especially for a terrier who's never really gotten to sink her teeth into anything substantial.''

Shelley's eyes flashed.

''Smart, in that case, would be knowing when to accept help,'' he said.

''Help? Or letting someone else seize control and make all the decisions? I've been down the handing - over - your - life - to - someone - else's - judgment route, Wayne, and let me tell you, it's not smart.''

This time he had nothing to say.

''I think taking charge of your own decisions, standing up for yourself and fighting your own dragons *is* smart.'' She folded her arms, rubbing her shoulder blade against the wall as she did. ''The truth is, you are not always going to be around to do those things, are you?''

''We've stopped talking about Tippie here, haven't we?''

''You tell me.''

They stood there at the foot of the stairs in stony

silence. He had no right to feel so possessive of her, no right to want to be responsible for her, no reason to resent both those feelings and worry that might someday consume him. But he felt all those things and so much more that he dared not speak for fear that all his emotions would come pouring out of him at once and overwhelm them both. He'd helped Shelley come this far, far enough to stand up to him and turn him away. He would not risk undoing that.

His resolve hardened like a rock in the pit of his stomach, and he clenched his jaw. "No."

"No what?" she asked softly, her eyes searching.

"No, we're not talking about Tippie anymore and, no, I won't always be around to rescue you."

"Good."

"What?"

"Because I neither want nor need rescuing." She jabbed one finger in his chest.

He could tell by the force and deadly aim of it that she'd wanted to do this for quite some time, but why? He'd only tried to help her, after all.

"I am perfectly capable of rescuing myself, should I require it—and of rescuing you, too, if the situation called for it."

He opened his mouth the second she paused to draw a breath, but a muffled sound from upstairs caught his attention. He put one hand on the rail and tipped his head to see if he heard it again.

"And if I make some mistakes, they are *my* mistakes to make, not your invitation to try to save me from myself,'' Shelley went on, oblivious to his actions.

There. He did hear it again, only louder this time. "Shelley—"

"Got it?"

"Shelley, I think—"

"Are you even listening to me?"

"No."

She stared at him slack-jawed, but he didn't have time to deal with that now. He headed up the stairs two at a time, saying as he went, "One of the twins is crying. I'm going to take care of it."

"Oh, no, you're not. The twins are my responsibility." He heard her footsteps pounding up the stairs behind him. "That's my dragon to slay."

"Not this time, princess." He blocked the door to the nursery where he could hear only faint sounds now. The twin must be quieting down.

"I have been baby-sitting for those girls since they were a few weeks old. You can't keep me from them now."

"I can if you haven't had chicken pox. That was the reason you asked me to come over, right? Because you weren't sure if you'd had chicken pox?"

She raised her hand as if intent on pushing him aside, then stopped.

He turned his head with his ear to the closed door and listened. All was quiet, but when he spoke, he still used a low whisper. "Why press

your luck? Let me take care of this. You take care
of Kyle and Maggie.''

She angled her chin. ''Let's just look at the list
of pros and cons here.''

''Oh, no, you're not going to start with the lists
again.''

''Number one—'' she held up her hand and
touched her index finger ''—if they have the
chicken pox, I have already been exposed because
I looked after them all day. Unless part of your
ability to save everyone from every stupid thing
they might ever do includes time travel, not even
you can change that.''

He relaxed his arm, braced across the nursery
door, just a bit.

''Two, if the girls are sick with anything from
the sniffles to the sub-Siberian dragon pox, they
are too tiny to understand why they feel so rotten
and will need a lot of...what did you call it? Comfort and aid?''

His hand slid lower on the door frame.

''Comfort and aid from someone they know and
trust.''

He shifted his weight.

''They will need help, and I am the one they
will need to give it to them. Surely you can understand that.''

He heaved a sigh and let his arm drop, but did
not move away from the door.

''Oh, c'mon, Wayne. You can't be this determined to control me that you'd—''

"Help."

"What?"

"I never wanted to control you." He held her gaze until he knew she'd let those words sink in; whether she believed them or not was another matter. "I only wanted to help you.'

"You wanted to rescue me. There's a difference."

He shook his head, not sure he understood.

"Wayne." She put her hand to his chest.

He shut his eyes. Her touch felt so good to him, like a homecoming he had longed for all his life.

"Much as I'd like to stand here and hash this all out with you, there are two children in there who may need me. If you really want to help and not control me, you'll stand aside and let me go to them."

"But I could just as easily do this for you, Shelley."

"And I want to do this for myself. It's not a huge deal, you know. And even if it isn't the smartest choice, it's mine to make, and the way you can help me is by not standing in my way."

Wayne gritted his teeth, exhaled hard through his nose, looked down, then at Shelley. At last he slowly pushed the door open and let her lead the way inside.

Chapter Eleven

"Celeste feels a little warm, but I think it's from having her blanket bunched up. She's drifted back to sleep now and Chelsea never even stirred." Shelley padded down the stairs toward Wayne, sitting on the bottom step. "I checked on Kyle and Maggie and they're totally zonked out."

"Congratulations. Looks like you've got your little ducks all in a row."

"Shouldn't that be dragons?" She stopped on the step above where he sat and nudged his thigh with her toe. When he didn't move over, she groaned and sat down where she was. "Okay, I have four of the children taken care of. Guess it's time to see what's wrong with the last one."

"Me? I'm childish? *Me?*"

"Ahh, it makes things so much simpler when

you just admit to it straight out like that.'' She slapped him on the back.

"Shelley, going in to take care of those kids when you don't know if it posed a personal risk was—''

"Just exactly the kind of thing you would have done.'' She bumped his shoulder with her knee.

He stared straight ahead.

She leaned back, enjoying the relief of scouring her itchy elbows on the thick carpet.

"You still shouldn't have done it.''

"But that's not your call, Wayne.''

"I just don't understand your resistance, Shelley. All I wanted to do was—''

"I know, I know, help me.''

"Build your confidence.'' He kept his back to her.

"What?''

"To prove to you that there are men around like me who you can count on and trust, because I knew you needed to trust a man again.''

"What are you saying, Wayne? That everything between us was just a means of manipulating me?''

"No.'' He looked at her over his shoulder. "Well...maybe. But when you say it like that, it sounds pretty lousy. I didn't do it to hurt you, Shelley. I did it—''

"Don't tell me, let me guess.'' She put her hand to her forehead. "You did it for my own good?''

"To help you.'' He said it with such quiet passion she almost forgave him on the spot. But she could not forgive him until she knew...

"Is that why you kissed me?"

"No." His eyes met hers. Regret and undisguised longing shone in his gaze, then he looked away. "The kisses were real. They were an impulse I probably should have resisted, for—"

"Don't." She could not bear to hear him say he should have resisted for her own good.

"It was wonderful, Shelley. I wanted to kiss you and kiss you again, then pick you up and carry you away and..." He cleared his throat and shifted on the step. "But a kiss is all that ever can be between us."

She started to touch his back, then stopped short. "Why?"

"Because I'm out of the rescuing-fair-maidens business." He stood and looked down at her, his expression somber but his eyes glinting with pain. "I spent too much of my time, wasted too much of my life, trying to save my mom and then my little sister from their own choices, to make up for all the damage my dad did to them. I was going to be the kind of man who never let them down. But in the end I did let them down."

"I can't believe that, Wayne."

"I must have. Why else would they have gone on making the same mistakes, my sister throwing herself into destructive relationship after destructive relationship? And my mom, staying with my dad through every kind of heartache and humiliation.''

"Those were their choices to make, Wayne. What could you have done?''

"I don't know.'' He shook his head. "If I'd just...'' He sighed. "Something. I should have done something more.''

"You told me once that as a lawyer you'd learned to be a good judge of human nature. Surely you know that no matter how much you did or tried to do without their cooperation, nothing would really change.''

He nodded. "My mind can accept that, but...'' he pounded his fist once to his chest "—when I think of my mom and sister and what they could have been and done with their lives, I can't help but think I should have done more.''

"That's what you were afraid would happen to me if I didn't start trusting that there were good men out there to be found? If I didn't let go of my past and move beyond my present behavior patterns?''

"Yes!'' He gave her arms a squeeze, his eyes shut in a show of ultimate relief. "Yes! That's it exactly. That's what I wanted to give you in the short time I knew we would have together.''

"You wanted to give me?'' She shot to her feet. Her voice rose. "*Give* me? Who the hell granted you that kind of power?''

"What?''

"The power to think you knew what was best

for me, then to believe you had the ability to give me a better life? Not to build a better life with me, or to work toward one, or even to search for one together. But to give it to me like...like...like a trophy on a platter?'' She jerked her chin up and folded her arms. ''You have your nerve—and a pretty screwed-up notion of what it means to help someone, to boot. Haven't you ever heard of the middle ground?''

''Have you?''

She blinked at him.

''Because I don't see much sign of it.'' His tone stayed steady, but the quiet power beneath his words grew with each point he made. ''You accuse me of trying to manipulate you and, heaven forbid, for your own welfare, but haven't you done the same to me? And for what other reason than you had to have your own way?''

''I was trying to keep from getting run over by the bulldozer you'd become trying to have everything *your* way.''

''Yeah, right. From the lists to the last-ditch attempt at seduction at the party. Lady, you have done nothing this whole week but try to get on top of me.''

She clutched her collar tightly over her neck.

''That is, get the better of me.'' He ran his hand back through his hair, and lowered his head. ''Of course, maybe we'd both be a little easier to live with if we'd tried the other thing.''

She fought back an unexpected shiver and

forced a cool shake of her head. "And to think I almost did."

His head still slightly bowed, he questioned her claim with the mere shift of his eyes.

"That's what I planned for us tonight, before the responsibility for the children was dropped in my lap. I had planned to go back to your house with you after the party and show you that I was capable of trusting a man again."

"Me."

"Maybe now you can understand why it blind-sided me so to learn tonight that you don't trust me, that you never trusted me to take care of myself and make the right decisions for my life without your expert guidance and intervention."

"Not trust you?" Hurt that she would suggest such a thing resounded in his words. He reached out and put his hand under her chin, then without force lifted her face until she was looking into his eyes.

She bit her lip to try to keep her natural response at bay but she'd acted too late. Her chest rose and fell in a slow longing sigh.

"Shelley, you are the brightest, most capable, most loyal—and, dammit, the sexiest woman I know." He moved closer on the step until their faces were so close she could feel his breath. "Not trust you? It's me I don't trust. I don't trust myself to measure up, to be the kind of man you need, to be worthy of caring for you, keeping up with you and loving you."

"Love?" The whisper hummed on her lips and reverberated through her being. "Wayne, are you saying—"

A child's cry kept her from finishing the question. Shelley wasn't sure if she felt remorse or relief at that, not sure if she could handle the answer, whatever it might be. Because even if Wayne did love her, they could never build a life together unless they found a way to stop seeing things as his way or her way.

A second child began to wail.

"You get that one, I'll get this one." Wayne pointed to Chelsea's crib as he made a beeline for Celeste's.

"My gosh, she's so hot." Shelley put her cheek to the scrunched-up face of the squalling toddler.

"Too hot." Wayne's huge hand covered the other child's forehead, his fingers tangling in the soft blond curls. "I think we'd better—"

"Get them out of these sleepers and wipe them down with a cool rag," she blurted, already heading for the door.

"Call the doctor," he finished, staying put right where he stood.

"Wayne, I know these kids and I know what's best for them."

"And I know there is a doctor just down the street who wouldn't mind dropping in to give his advice." He held Celeste to his chest and stopped to make soothing cooing sounds to her even as he headed out the door. "I'll call him from the master bedroom."

"Wayne, we're not dealing with choosing a wedding veil here. You can't just disregard my opinion on this, and I don't think it's anywhere near time to call a doctor in."

He stopped just outside the door to the master bedroom. "You're right. It should be your decision, Shelley. Tell me how I can best help, princess."

Both twins had quieted, and Celeste had even laid her head on Wayne's shoulder and began sucking her thumb. He put his cheek to the top of her head. Whether it was a gesture of comfort or to test the baby's temperature she did not know or care. The sight went straight to her heart and for the first time opened her eyes to the real goodness in this man. He had only wanted to help all along, and he'd done it because…because he loved her.

And she loved him. It scared the stuffing out of her to imagine it, but it was true. She loved Wayne Perry.

"You can help by making that call." She walked toward him, pausing as she got to his side. "We'll lay the twins on the bed so I can get them out of these sleepers while you do."

"You mean, we'll work together? A little bit your way, a little bit mine?"

"It's a crazy idea, I know. But it just might work." She tossed him a smile as she passed.

"You know, it just might, after all."

* * *

"I now pronounce you husband and wife. You may kiss your bride."

Wayne gave the preacher a nod of thanks, then turned to face his bride. His fingers fumbled at first, trying to lift the flimsy layer of sparkling veil that covered Shelley's beautiful face. It snagged on the glittering tiara on top of her softly waving hair. He frowned and started to try to work it free when her hand met his.

"Here, let me help you with that." In one fluid gesture they swept the fabric back together. Then Shelley went up on tiptoe.

Wayne took her face in both hands.

She smiled.

He tipped his head and brought his mouth to hers. Just before he kissed her, he grinned and murmured something she'd said the first time he'd ever laid eyes on her. "And they lived happily ever after."

"You bet your white knight they did," she replied, and met his promise-filled kiss with her own.

* * * * *